D0387041

Praise for *An Endless Christmas*

"In *An Endless Christmas*, the characters walked right off those pages and into my heart, setting up residence and bringing along all the joy and peace they had learned. I love Christmas novellas, and this one is now in my top three of favorites through the years."

Lauraine Snelling, award-winning, best-selling author of more than 80 books, including *An Untamed Heart*

"*An Endless Christmas* offers up a banquet of faith, family, and new beginnings, perfect for the season of hope."

Lisa Wingate, national best-selling author of *The Sea Keeper's Daughters*

"With her trademark wit and keen insight into what makes love last, Cynthia takes us on a jovial ride through the pages of *An Endless Christmas.*"

Robin Jones Gunn, best-selling author of *Finding Father Christmas*

"*An Endless Christmas* is the perfect Christmas story. A warm-fire tale of family, traditions, friendship, and love. And healing. Ruchti's smooth prose and voice evoke a Christmas warmth on the pages, and in our hearts. A story to be savored. A story to keep."

Rachel Hauck, *USA Today* best-selling author of *The Wedding Dress* and *How To Catch A Prince*

"Read *An Endless Christmas*. And then you'll want to read it again and again. Enjoying Cynthia Ruchti's book has now become as much a part of my Christmas traditions as cherishing my mother's collection of Dickens carolers."

Eva Marie Everson, best-selling, award-winning author of *Five Brides*

"*An Endless Christmas* is guaranteed to pull at your heartstrings and leave a lifelong impression of family, unconditional love, and God's redemptive power."

Cristel Phelps, Mount Hope Church, Lansing, MI

"Cynthia magically weaves one of the most inspiring contemporary Christmas tales with gentle lessons and examples that we all should follow; all the while revealing a poignant love story through several generations. This Christmas story will be reread and enjoyed every Christmas season."

Dianne Burnett, former Christianbook.com fiction editor

"Sweet and fun and sweet and moving and sweet and tender and funny and touching and . . . sweet! All of that in one *An Endless Christmas* experience. I closed the book with a contented smile—and with the thought that I could SO read this one again."

Rhonda Rhea, TV personality, humor columnist, author of *Turtles in the Road, Espresso Your Faith* and many more

"*An Endless Christmas* by Cynthia Ruchti runs true to form for this very talented writer. Delightful read!"

Kathi Macias, award-winning author of *Return to Christmas*

"Cynthia has related for us, in story fashion, the importance of family and boundless love. Even if we are 'orphans' we are part of the endless family of God—loved and cherished forever as His children."

Deb Haggerty, editor, speaker, writer at PositiveGrace.com

"Few books bring out the soul of strong family ties and being blessed in whatever God allows the way *An Endless Christmas* did. The story grabbed me from the very first chapter and held me captive until the final page."

Jill Swanson, image coach, author, speaker

"There is an incomparable charm in the way Cynthia Ruchti puts words on paper. And when she tells the story of *An Endless Christmas*, she captures the heart of this beloved holiday. The characters and the story are authentic and honest. You'll find yourself wishing for your own never-ending Yuletide."

Karen Porter, international speaker, author, and coach

"*An Endless Christmas* is a story of endless love—not the unrealistic fairytale kind of love, but the kind that endures and perseveres through difficult times, the kind of love that forges a path of forgiveness for future generations to follow."

Becky Melby, author of the *Lost Sanctuary* Series

"Reading Cynthia Ruchti's fiction is like playing *Clue*—looking for the threads and psychological hints that intertwine characters and lead to unanticipated outcomes. Her fiction—like *An Endless Christmas*—is an invitation to explore the settings that shape her characters."

Rachel Mantik, Church library specialist,
English and reading specialist

"*An Endless Christmas* has an endless message—one of hope, healing, and the unconditional love of family. This book reminds us that the things that really matter in life are not tangible; they are found in the hearts and lives of those we love."

Linda Gilden, author of *Mama Was the Queen of Christmas*

"Cynthia Ruchti did it again. She captured my interest, drew me into her characters' lives, caused me to marvel at her clever use of words, and kept me cycling between smiles and sobs. It's a story delightfully wrapped in the sights, sounds, celebration, and significance of the season. Enjoy it! I sure did."

Twila Belk (aka The Gotta Tell Somebody Gal),
speaker and author of six books, including *Raindrops from Heaven*

"*An Endless Christmas* captured my heart and my imagination. Thank you Cynthia Ruchti for introducing me to the folks on the pages of this book. And thank you for reminding me of the importance—not the perfection—of family."

Kendra Smiley, conference speaker and author of *Heart Clutter: Sifting Through the Contents of My Heart, Mind, and Memory*

"With her usual warmth, piercing insights into the human heart and quirky characters, Ruchti creates a world where the 'no matter what' love of Christ is demonstrated. Grab a cup of cocoa and some tissues to best enjoy this one!"

Sue Badeau, author of *Are We There Yet: The Ultimate Road Trip Adopting and Raising 22 Kids*, speaker and adoptive parent

"Grab a cup of hot cocoa and settle in for a charming Christmas story brimming with all the joy and hope of the season. *An Endless Christmas* is the perfect holiday gift for Ms. Ruchti's many fans."

Dorothy Love, author of *A Respectable Actress*

"*An Endless Christmas* is a charming and heart-warming story of Christmas as we wish it to be. Loved it!"

Gayle Roper, author of *Seaside Gifts, Lost and Found*

"*An Endless Christmas* provides readers with that touch of home and love and family most of us are looking for during the holiday season. Something that will make us think a little and love a lot."

Wanda Erickson, librarian

"Author Cynthia Ruchti once again reveals her adept skill in crafting a story of a family's welcoming warmth—enough to thaw the chill of any doubt or fear."

Kathy Carlton Willis, women's ministry leader and author of *Grin with Grace*

An Endless Christmas

CYNTHIA RUCHTI

Published by Worthy Inspired, an imprint of Worthy Publishing Group, a division of Worthy Media, Inc., One Franklin Park, 6100 Tower Circle, Suite 210, Franklin, TN 37067.

Helping people experience the heart of God

eBook available wherever digital books are sold.

Library of Congress Cataloging-in-Publication Data

Ruchti, Cynthia.
An endless Christmas : a novella / Cynthia Ruchti.
pages ; cm
Summary: "Award-winning novelist's heartwarming story about family and love lost, found, and finally truly revealed at Christmas"-- Provided by publisher.
ISBN 978-1-61795-587-7 (hardcover)
1. Man-woman relationships--Fiction. 2. Marriage proposals--Fiction. 3. Families--Fiction. 4. Christmas stories. 5. Domestic fiction. I. Title.
PS3618.U3255E53 2015
813'.6--dc23
2015022519

ISBN 978-1-61795-587-7

Cover Design by Chris Gilbert / Studio Gearbox

Printed in the United States of America

1 2 3 4 5—LBM—19 18 17 16 15

TO THE FAMILY THAT
INSPIRES ME EVERY DAY

For tonight darkness fell
into the dawn of love's light.*

*from the song "All Is Well," Michael W. Smith/Wayne Kirkpatrick, Published by

CHAPTER ONE

"*WHAT* DID SHE SAY?"

A carol played in the background. Carols perpetually played in the background at the Binders' cottage at Christmas, Katie Vale had quickly learned. The music almost covered the whispered "What did she say?" that made the rounds of the room built for two that now held twenty.

"She said no." Dodie Binder—matriarch and tone-setter—leaned closer to her husband, Wilson, whose smile collapsed, stroke-like, when she repeated the answer in his good ear.

"She said no?" He wasn't the only one asking for clarification.

Katie fingered the heirloom ring. In her hand, not on it. A square-cut diamond surrounded by tiny sapphires. A narrow, glitter-edged ribbon looped through its circle. Moments earlier it had hung on the Binders' tinseled Christmas tree. "I said . . ."—she apologized to Micah Binder with her eyes and with all she couldn't express—"no. I can't accept this. I can't—"

Was it her imagination, or did the room tilt when all the Binder women shifted to where she stood, wrapping their sweatered and fleeced arms around her, even the youngest? The eight-year-old. What was her name again?

If she'd had more than ten minutes to meet the family before Micah drew her to the Christmas tree and the one ornament out of character with the others, she might have remembered. Twilight. That was her name. The girl who hugged her around the middle as if grabbing on to a teddy bear after falling off her bike.

All Katie wanted to do was apologize properly to Micah, to explain why she had to say no. But the chaos of comfort kept them apart. She caught a glimpse of Micah's face—iconic for the word *crestfallen*—in a sea of three uncles and his dad.

She closed her hand around the ring to keep it from slipping to the floor in the melee of "It'll be okay" and "Don't you worry, now" and "All is well."

"All Is Well." Really? That's the Christmas song that decided now was a good time to make its presence known?

A voice with the timbre of an eighty-year-old woman—must be Grandma Dodie—said something that sounded a lot like, "Good for you, honey."

Should she worry or feel blessed that the Binder women gathered around her like professional mourners? Mourners with sweet smiles, no tears. Curious. She dug in and inched closer to Micah, who sat on the arm of the couch where he'd landed after she refused his proposal. The crowd of huggers moved with her like a swarm of shiny fish that swim in circles through the sea.

Micah. He didn't deserve what he was probably going through right now. "Can we talk?" she mouthed, peeking between two of Micah's aunts. If his heart ached like hers did . . .

Before he could answer, an earsplitting sound pierced through the supposed-to-be-soothing Christmas music. A smoke detector.

"To the kitchen!" Grandma Dodie shouted. "You little ones stay back." She gave Katie one final squeeze. "It's tradition to char at least one pan of cookies every year. Let's assume that's all this is." She limped behind the uncles, who raced past her. They called out the "Not to worry. We've got it under control" before she made it through the kitchen door.

One of the college-aged grandkids—Bella? Elisa?—rounded up the younger ones and steered them to the overflowing pegs of coats and boots lined up near the front door. "Outside, kiddies. Let's go get the mail, okay?"

It took seven people to get the mail? None of the children objected. Within minutes they were out the door as if on an epic adventure. Micah and Katie were the only two left in the family room. It adjoined the kitchen in Dodie and Wilson's small cottage in the woods, but the other adults had formed a hedge of noise between the two rooms, leaving the couple virtually alone.

"Micah, I—"

He raised his hand to stop her. "No explanation necessary."

"You're okay with this?" Maybe she'd overestimated his affection for her. Good to know.

"Not okay." He tapped his heart with a closed fist. "But you don't have to say anything. No is an answer."

"But it isn't the whole story."

He stood then and stepped close enough to plant his hands on her shoulders. "Katie?" The tremor in his voice and the look in his eyes told the truth. He wasn't brushing off her rejection as if it didn't matter. Those pale blue eyes that had at first startled her, then captivated her, blinked back man-tears. "I . . ."

"What is it?" Would she have the resolve to refuse if he asked again? It was for his own good. If only he knew that. *God, a little help here?*

Micah's forehead became as rutted as the snow-packed lane that had brought them to the cottage. He opened his mouth, then closed it again. A deep breath. "I'll show you where you can put your things. You get the window seat in the kitchen. It's not as bad as it sounds. Pretty roomy, actually, and more than long enough for . . . the petite." He headed toward the luggage they'd left near the front door in Micah's haste to move straight from, "Hi, everyone. This is Katie Vale," to "Katie, will you marry me?"

"I can't stay," she said. He couldn't think she would stay there at the cottage with the family whose favorite—and only—male grandchild she'd just jilted, could he?

He turned to face her, eyes wide. “Do you want me out of your life?”

“No!”

Micah smiled. “That ‘no’ stung a lot less than the first one.”

The man was not right in the head. Better to find out now.

He opened the front closet and slid her luggage into the only horizontal shelf space not already occupied. “You’ll have to tuck your carry-on into the storage cubby under the window seat. Just lift off the cushion and you’ll find a hinged lid. Your blankets and pillow are in there, too, Grandma Dodie said.”

She was staying? No. Talk about awkward family gatherings. She thought she’d seen them all.

“Did I hear my name used in vain?” Grandma Dodie poked her head around the corner between the family room and kitchen.

Micah waved her into the room. “I was explaining the intricacies of finding sleeping accommodations for a crowd this large.”

“We’re all set for you, Katie. Your towels are the pink ones in the bathroom to the right.”

“Why is no one booting me out the door?” She kept her voice as light as possible, under the circumstances.

“Oh, honey,” Dodie said. “You don’t want to miss the Binder Family Christmas. Does she, Micah?”

“I wouldn’t, if I were her.” He walked past Katie and whispered, “It’ll be okay. Promise.”

How, how, how could it be okay? And how had they gone from wheels down in the Minneapolis/St. Paul airport to this new episode in the chronicles of Katie's failed relationships?

TWO HOURS EARLIER

Katie slid her phone into her purse, the flesh of her heart still smoking from the way the texted words burned.

"Anything important?" Micah asked, glancing only briefly from his position behind the steering wheel of the economy rental car.

Important? A death knell. "It can wait."

"You really are trying to unplug from work this week, aren't you? Proud of you," he said. "If I hadn't forgotten my charger, the challenge would be harder for me. Battery will last maybe through the rest of the day. Then I'm turning Amish. Unless somebody at the cottage has a charger to match. They have to. Won't last long, though, with Grandma's house rules."

What did that mean?

He pointed to the dash display. "Hey, look. The temp has dropped another two degrees. We're now officially sixty degrees colder than we would be at home right now."

Katie rubbed her jean-covered knees and wiggled her toes in her new-enough-to-be-stiff fleece-lined boots, as if the rental car's heater wasn't adequate to ward off the chill threatening outside the vehicle. December in the Northwoods. Stunning in pictures. Frostbite waiting to happen, up close and personal. Her Southern roots were showing. "I'm not sure I'm ready for this."

Micah reached for the heater control.

She stopped him with a gloved hand over his. "It's not the weather." Katie leaned her head against the passenger-side window. Cold as an ice pack but without its pain-reducing effects. Even if she could discount the hollowing text message, who wouldn't feel at least mild apprehension at the thought of meeting "the parents" for the first time?

Meeting Micah's parents at Christmas meant meeting the whole Binder family—his grandparents, cousins, aunts, uncles . . . Everybody except Micah's sister Courtney and her husband, Brogan—the two closest to their own age—who had an excused absence. They waited in a South Korean hotel for the final processing of their international adoption.

Family tradition—the can't-miss Christmas Week extravaganza at the grandparents' cottage north of Stillwater.

She should have turned him down, should have told Micah she'd use a vacation week for the meet-the-parents challenge some other time, when she'd only have two names to remember and a smaller tangle of relationships to navigate. Christmas Week with all the family appendages present? This could only end badly. Especially now, when she was on the verge of saying the words that should have been said months ago.

If Binder family traditions followed the Vale reputation, somehow the fingers would point to Katie when it all fell apart.

Case in point. She was free to follow Micah to Minnesota because her own parents had bailed on her. As if their passive-aggressive divorce wasn't enough of a barrier to a Currier and Ives Christmas, they'd both called at the last minute to cancel their individual plans with her. No awkward dinner out with her dad and his smartphone. No post-Christmas, unnecessary shopping excursion with her let's-make-up-for-everything-by-buying-us-both-a-new-purse mother.

"Katie?"

She tugged her thoughts back to the question at hand. "The flight tired me out more than I thought, I guess."

"We could still be stuck in Fort Myers or Atlanta if they hadn't gotten the remnants of this last snow cleared so fast. Minnesota sure knows how to move snow."

He meant that as a comfort, right? It sounded as if he considered snow removal an Olympic event. Stuck in sunny Fort Myers sounded pretty good at the moment, empty Christmas or not.

The road from the Minneapolis/St. Paul airport to Stillwater had narrowed from six lanes to four to two as their destination neared. Micah insisted the scenic St. Croix Trail—Highway 95—would be worth the extra time. She didn't mind dragging out the inevitable.

On the map app, the St. Croix River sported a seam down its middle, a dotted line drawn by cartographers with loyalties to Minnesota's rights to the waterway on the west and Wisconsin's on the east. Katie rubbed at an invisible dotted line on her forehead. Cartographers? Her territory-war parents. The line bit deeper the closer she and Micah neared Stillwater.

"You're not worried about meeting my family, are you?" Micah had the pecan-pie-rich voice of a radio announcer without the affectation. Soothing whether he meant it that way or not.

Katie sensed her heart rate slow in response to his words. Or his tone. Or the fact that he cared. "Meeting them isn't the problem. Meeting them at Christmas seems . . . serious."

Trees flashed past the car window like warp-speed time-keepers. *This is it. The moment he realizes you're not worth fighting for. They all do. My parents included. Worth fighting over. Not worth fighting for.*

How many hash marks would tick by before he said something?

Serious. She'd said it sounded serious. *Bad call, Katie.* It no longer surprised her when relationships collapsed. But this one? The threat of losing Micah? She couldn't dodge the text's revelation about her genealogy, as if that were her only concern. It would come to light sooner or later. The sting sliced through her like a laser torch through steel. That would leave a permanent scar.

Micah pulled on to the apron of a plowed driveway, easing the car farther off the road than the snow-packed shoulders would have allowed. He killed the engine and faced her. "Katie, if you're that uncomfortable, we'll turn around and head back to the city. I can get you a hotel room near the airport while we figure out an earlier flight home."

How did he do that? Make his voice as mellow as peach blossom honey even on a subject like this one? He was willing to sacrifice the week he hadn't stopped talking about since before Thanksgiving?

She looked past him, to the right of his disarmingly tender smile. Snowing again. The flakes floating more than falling. If only she could master that technique. "I don't want to be responsible for your missing Christmas with your grandparents."

He shook his head as if that had never been a consideration. "I'll drive up alone after we work out your flight change. I can't miss this Christmas. It might be their last." His face had lost its normal guileless confidence.

He stroked the side of her face with the backs of his fingers, then leaned in to kiss the same spot. "Meeting my family is not for the faint of heart. Or for a woman who isn't sure she wants to be there. With me."

How could he think this was about him? She was the high-risk half of their relationship. Wasn't it obvious? She was the one genetically predisposed to messing up anything remotely promising. Wait. He'd said, "It might be their last." Why hadn't he mentioned that earlier? "Their last Christmas?"

"Maybe." He leaned back against the driver's seat, hands now on the steering wheel, eyes forward. "Could be for any of us, couldn't it?"

On another guy, the expression might have seemed contrived. A guilt-producer designed to change her mind. But Micah didn't operate that way. He could teach seminars on integrity. And he was clearly hurting. Or thinking ahead to life without one of his grandparents.

She had to be there. Whether she was ready or not. Katie could bear a week of emotional discomfort. She'd mastered the art in twenty-nine years as the daughter of parents who ate conflict for breakfast. Stillwater was as good a place as any to hide from the inevitable. She had to be there. Not just with him but for him. He needed someone to lean on. She wanted it to be her.

Before pulling back onto the highway, Micah checked his phone. "Oh."

"What?"

"We have to kill some time in Stillwater."

She shifted in her seat. "Why?"

"We're waiting for Twilight."

"Won't it be harder to find the place after it gets dark?"

"Twilight, my cousin. Eight years old. Her final performance in the *Nutcracker Suite* was this afternoon. They're hightailing it from White Bear Lake but haven't arrived yet."

"I don't understand why we can't—"

Micah replaced his phone. He rubbed the steering wheel as if the genie inside would grant him the right words. "I wanted everybody to be there when you walk in."

With the engine off, the air temp in the car had dropped dramatically. But his words and tenderness spread warmth through her like a Bradenton Beach sun.

"You're a remarkable man, Micah." She ran one finger—feather-soft—across the back of his neck. His love language.

He caught her hand in his. "You made me this way. I was a complete louse until you came into my life." He started the engine. "And if you believe that," he said, flicking ashes from an imaginary Groucho Marx cigar . . .

He'd done it again—gotten her to shrug the concern from her shoulders and laugh in spite of herself.

"So how will we kill time in Backwater, Minnesota?" She flicked her own imaginary cigar.

"Stillwater, my dear." He maintained his Groucho Marx improv. "We could get a cup of coffee or tea. Or I could show you around town." Back to her Micah again.

Hers. She'd better be careful with thoughts like that. Disappointment fed on impossibilities. "Sounds good to me."

"You know what Einstein always said."

Katie tried to ignore signs of civilization reappearing along the roadsides and focus on Micah's camera-friendly profile. "Despite memorizing most of what Einstein wrote, I'm not sure about the quote to which you refer."

Micah cleared his throat. "'The only thing you absolutely have to know is the location of the library.' And Stillwater's is exceptional, by the way. Rooftop terrace, stained-glass windows, wrought-iron shelving. A 1901 Carnegie project. A work of art. Or architecture, which is art."

Laughter came easily and often when she was with him. "Coffee first, okay?"

"Done."

Within minutes, they'd driven through Bayport. A small, industrial-looking town with a window/patio door factory and a correctional facility, which seemed to embrace polar opposite visions. Bayport's marina housed hundreds of shrink-wrapped boats, many larger than Katie's condo even if you included the lanai.

Bayport's city limits hadn't faded from view when they were greeted by a "Welcome to Stillwater" sign. "Birthplace of Minnesota," it said.

"Really?" she said. "Birthplace of Minnesota?" They were spending Christmas in the Bethlehem of the Northwoods?

"Also voted one of the prettiest small towns in America by *Forbes*." Micah braked for a slow-moving vehicle ahead of them and matched the pace. "I appreciate those facts," he said, "but when I think of Stillwater, I think of—"

"What?"

"Family."

He'd said the word as if it was the final line of a classic poem. More proof of how different their life experiences had been. How many times had she been able to use that word without flinching?

They rounded a bend at the spot where a sheer rock face and shallow caves edged the western side of the street and a half-dozen 1880s-era paddlewheel boats snugged the shoreline of the St. Croix on their right. When had the traffic grown so thick? Katie blessed the traffic congestion for slowing their pace so she could take in what she was seeing.

"This came out of nowhere," she said, gesturing to the main street as it opened before them.

"Always seems that way to me too. Pretty stunning, especially at this time of year with the Christmas lights and decorations."

"No wonder you're partial to this place, Micah." She scanned the architecture of the buildings lining the street.

"The whole commercial district is listed in the National Register of Historic Places."

"For a guy who stops at every historic landmark . . ."

Micah glanced her way. "You said you found that charming about me."

"I do. Quirky, but charming."

They approached a stoplight. Micah took the opportunity to direct her attention to the way the streets to the left of the main street—conveniently named Main Street—climbed at a steep incline away from the downtown area. "Can you imagine navigating those inclines when they're iced over?"

A long block later, Micah turned onto a side street that approached the river and whooped over the joy of finding an empty parking space. "You'd think this would be the off season, but Christmas Week is crazy-busy in Stillwater. Lots happening."

Katie imagined how the lights would look against the dark of night. Even at this hour, they made the town glisten. Small Christmas trees sat in barrel-sized clay pots with bunches of red berries snugged among their branches. Dancing snow added to the picturesque scene.

Micah slid around the car to open her door for her. "Come on. Let's see if we can get into LoLo's."

"LoLo's is . . . ?"

"Locally Owned. Locally Operated. Locally sourced, too, I think. When possible. You'll love the smoked salmon."

She raced to keep up with his energy. "We're only having coffee, aren't we? Your grandmother would give you 'what for' if we spoiled our supper."

"So, you've met her?"

"Assumed."

"It's a smoked salmon tasting plate. The size of a cucumber slice. I don't think there's much danger we'll ruin our appetites for supper."

She slipped her arm through the crook of Micah's elbow. "Can we slow down a notch?"

"Sorry. Sure."

"I haven't seen you this animated in the nine months we've been dating. Ten." Valentine's Day. Normally the worst day for a first date. Turned out to be her best decision ever.

Micah stopped walking and faced her. "My favorite

season. My favorite place." He brushed a snowflake or two from her hair. "My . . . favorite." He let the word hang in the sparkling air.

They'd become a sidewalk hazard.

"We'd better—" She nodded in the direction they'd been heading.

"Right. LoLo's." He tucked her hand into his elbow again and led her through the crowd to a glass-front building where Olive Street teed into Main and the crosswalk led right to the front door. "After you."

They took the last free table—a high top tucked into the window nook. Every false expectation about "backwater" dissolved into the ambiance of the tin ceiling, Edison light fixtures, and the menu that read like an episode from the Food Network. Chicken curry soup. Korean barbecue skirt steak wraps. Bacon jam crostini.

They ordered coffee and the smoked salmon tasting plates, then turned their attention to the activity on the sidewalks.

"With the Twin Cities so close," Micah said, "this is a prime destination for weekend getaways or events like the jazz fest, the art festival, balloon fest . . ."

"Why haven't you talked about Stillwater more? You seem content in Florida. Aside from despising your job."

He played teeter-totter with his fork. "I don't despise my job."

She tilted her head and waited.

"No more than you do yours."

She smoothed the linen napkin in her lap. Her restlessness wasn't tied to job dissatisfaction as strongly as Micah's. The position she held had its rewarding moments. "Thought I was hiding that better."

"Work is work. It's not always how we want to spend the rest of our lives, though."

No wonder he'd downplayed his promotions and awards. "So, Stillwater?"

"When my grandpa retired from working at the power plant, everyone expected them to move to Arizona or Texas." Micah drew imaginary lines on the black tabletop, from where they were to southwest of the salt grinder.

"Or Florida," she added.

"Right. Instead, they bought the cottage they have now so they could stay centrally located to their kids and grandkids."

"Except you."

"We have to go where the job takes us sometimes. And, to its credit, it led me to you." He reached across the table for her hand. "Fresh-squeezed orange juice, year-round farmer's markets, and you."

When her Vale genetics showed their relationship ineptitude, when he realized the ten months they'd had together were about to come to an end, he'd be left with fresh OJ and Plant City strawberries. Even with innumerable beaches within driving distance, would that be enough to hold him in Florida? When had a beach sunset created the kind of excitement she read in his eyes now as Micah peered through the restaurant window at the activity on Stillwater's Main Street?

Micah, what do you really want? Where would you live if you could? You're winning commendations in medical supply sales, but that isn't your true heart. Your workplace isn't to blame. It's the whole career choice.

He pointed with a little boy's excitement to a small, horse-drawn wagon making its way down the crowded, snow-dusted street. Now wasn't the right time to talk about life goals.

Bolstered with coffee and Katie's growing curiosity about their destination, and armed with an "all clear" from Micah's uncle, they left the restaurant and navigated the rest of Stillwater's Main Street. Their northern trajectory took them out of town and into an eclectic countryside of high class subdivisions tucked in the spaces between sandstone cliffs, simple farms, brief glimpses of the St. Croix, and cedar- and birch-lined pastureland.

Five miles from the edge of town, Micah signaled. Katie saw no side road. It wasn't snowing that hard. Visibility was good enough to see the forest for the trees. Should she mention that he'd bumped his turn signal? They'd said little to each other since pulling back onto 95. She'd made temporary peace with herself about spending Christmas Week with his family.

He seemed to have picked up the nerves she'd dropped on his behalf. Micah sighed as he slowed and followed his signal onto a narrow path between pines and hardwoods.

"Hold on," he said. "The last road to be plowed after a snowfall."

"Is this even a road?" Katie gripped the handhold above the passenger window. Two tire-wide indentations in the four inches of snow looked more like a ski trail.

Micah told her its name, his voice distorted by his laughter.

"Lover's Lane? You're taking me down Lover's Lane on the way to your grandparents' cottage? Micah!"

He focused on keeping the car's tires in the tracks and between the trees, not among them. "Lubber's. Lubber's Lane. No one knows if it was named for a guy named Lubber or a commentary on the fact that it angles away from the St. Croix rather than closer to it. Land lubbers. Maybe it was an 1800s version of a typo. Lumber/lubber."

"There's the other option."

"What's that?"

Katie braced herself on the console with her other hand as they bounced over something more solid than snow. "The county road commissioner fought a nasty head cold the day he named it. 'I nobinate this stretch ob road Lubber's—'"

"You have to tell that to my uncle Paul, Katie. That's his kind of humor."

Uncles and aunts and cousins and Micah's mom and dad and his grandparents and nieces and . . . She stole back some of the anxiety she'd relinquished earlier. She had dibs.

Be anxious for nothing. Not the typical Christmas season reading. Philippians? For Christmas Week? She'd packed the narrow devotional book into her checked luggage. No way to reach it now and remind herself why God thought "for nothing" applied to her.

"If you're wondering if they'll like you"—Micah seemed to read her thoughts—"you have nothing to fear. I told them"—major steering wheel correction—"that you could charm the scales off a bluegill and make it fry itself up just to be helpful."

"You got that phrase from your uncle Paul, didn't you?"

Micah risked a glance at her before focusing again on Lubber's Lane. "I may have picked up a nugget or two of wisdom from him."

She admired Micah's ability to rebound from the earlier pall of sadness about how little time his grandparents might have left on earth. Possibly their last Christmas together. What would it be like to live with that threat coloring their celebration? Even her own tabled problems were trumped by that.

The houses sat farther apart in this stretch. The road, snow-packed as it was, signaled civilization. Little else did. They passed houses that intimidated with their extravagant size. Katie shuddered with thoughts of mortgages and taxes—never a pleasant subject for her. On their left sat a pair of farmhouses that drooped with age and disrepair. Micah kept driving. Katie exhaled her gratitude.

"How much farther?"

"Until we get there."

"Very funny."

A split-rail fence with an evergreen wreath at every junction framed a scene that captured Katie's attention. Micah slowed as if knowing how much she would want to soak in the scene before they continued their journey. A low, cranberry-red house sat far off the road with a long stretch of unbroken white between it and the fence. Candles in each window. A wreath on the wide front door.

"Micah, stop!"

"Now? Here?" He braked and slid the transmission into Park. "If that's what you want." His voice sounded a tad bit patronizing. She ignored the inflection.

"I want to get a picture of this. Do you mind?" She pulled her phone from her coat pocket and powered down the window. After several clicks, she let the window return to its job of blocking some of the biting cold. "Thank you." She scrolled through the images she'd captured on her phone. "I love this shot." She held the screen toward him. "Perfect Christmas scene, isn't it? Thanks for indulging me."

"Not a problem. Can we go now?"

She pocketed her camera and took one last look at the dream scene, her nose pressed against the glass, fogging it more with each exhale. "Yes."

Micah accelerated slowly but the car skidded as it fought to regain momentum. A handful of seconds later, he pulled the car into the driveway at the end of the line of wreathed fencing.

"I got the pictures I wanted, Micah. We'll get in trouble if we drive in any farther. Micah, stop!" She tugged on the sleeve of his Columbia fleece while watching the cranberry cottage for signs of life. Or a shotgun. Or a security system floodlight. Not yet dusk, but a floodlight would scare off most intruders, wouldn't it?

Micah kept navigating the well-plowed driveway. "Wave to the nice lady, Katie."

"What?"

He pointed to the round, haloed face peeking through the nearest window. "That's my Grandma Dodie."

CHAPTER TWO

THE RING STILL CLUTCHED in her palm, Katie now stood alone in the cottage's family room. The tree's ornaments shone a repeated message of balsam-scented joy-joy-joy, echoed in the ever-present music soundtrack. Laughter from the kitchen told her a pan of burnt cookies hadn't dampened anyone's spirit of celebration. The kids'—all girls—trip to the mailbox stretched much longer than the driveway. Judging from the sounds drifting from outside, they'd found some way to turn their assignment into a giggle fest. Katie slipped the ring into the pocket of her quilted vest for safekeeping until she could return it. To the man she loved.

Micah had disappeared, probably hanging out with the uncles and his dad. They, too, moved as a pack.

How long could Katie hide in the bathroom? She'd disappointed a whole, wide, stick-together-through-thick-and-thicker family in addition to the finest man who'd ever crossed her path. The finest. For the last seven of the ten months they'd been dating, she imagined the two of them as a forever couple. Longed for it to work. Prayed for a chance to prove marriage didn't have to look like the one her parents butchered.

She needed a minute in the bathroom. And not just as a hiding place.

Uncle Paul's wife—Allie, she was pretty sure—met her as Katie headed down the hall to search. "Bathroom?" Katie asked her.

"Two doors down, on the right." Allie smiled at her. "Jiggle the handle of the toilet."

Two doors. On the right. There. Wait just a minute. A schedule? To the left of the doorway hung a whiteboard schedule for bathroom time. Seriously? She supposed it would be tough coordinating showers and other necessities for twenty-plus people for the week. But, a schedule? She visually scrolled through, looking for her name. A block of time from five ten to five fifteen p.m. It was one minute after five. A slot reserved for Grandma Dodie.

The bathroom was empty. It would only take Katie a minute or two. How did an eighty-year-old woman adhere to a schedule like this?

Katie had caused enough trouble. She wasn't about to bend the restroom rules her first day too. She retraced her steps and found the kitchen crew. "Mrs. Binder?"

Four women answered, "Yes?"

"Grandma Binder?"

She looked up from stirring something on the stove in the white and mint green retro kitchen. "What is it, dear?"

Katie drew a deep breath. "Can I trade you my five ten for your five o'clock? In the bathroom?"

The kitchen stilled. Morgue-still. Even the bubbling on the stove quieted. Then the room erupted in laughter.

"We got her!"

"Never grows old, does it?"

"Wait until the guys hear."

"Micah was right. She's impeccably kind and considerate."

Grandma Dodie planted her hands on her more than adequate hips. "You girls are as bad as your husbands. Katie, child, go on. The schedule's only for showers. And that's just to give the hot water heater a break."

In unison, the women called after her, "We're sorry!"

"No, you're no-ot," Katie sing-songed in return.

More giggling. "Good thing we videotaped her reaction for the guys," one of them said.

Katie stopped. They wouldn't have. Couldn't have. But there it was. On a small shelf right above the whiteboard in the hallway—a baby cam trained on where she stood outside the door. She entered the bathroom and closed the door a little harder than necessary. If this was their idea of revenge against her for— No, they wouldn't have had time to rig all that. And Micah hadn't hinted they were the revengeful sort.

This was her initiation into the family. She'd said no to him, but still had to run the gauntlet. In a family that forgave her without blinking.

Game on.

Katie would have checked the text from the genealogy resource again, but the Binder cottage was a technology-free zone for the duration of Christmas Week. Landline only. Cell phones, tablets, e-readers, iPads, gaming systems were collected on arrival and kept in a sealed bin.

She supposed she could have objected, as a non-family member. But the text was burned into her brain. Staring at it again wouldn't change its message. She'd have to show it and the rest of her ancestry research to Micah eventually. It would help him understand. Or maybe not. How could someone who came from Binder stock understand?

Everywhere she looked, she saw evidence of investment in the idea of family longevity. Photo albums on the shelves in the hall. Framed pictures. Children's handmade ornaments on the tree dating to past decades. The adults gave the impression they loved and cared for their nieces as much as their own children. Husbands and wives sitting close, holding hands, serving one another.

And she'd been there less than an hour.

The women were still congregated in the kitchen. That's where she should be. Helping, not avoiding the inevitable.

"Can we talk?" She braved a discussion that held the potential to make her homeless for the week. Or ostracized for a lifetime.

The kitchen chatter quieted, except for the hum of the dishwasher.

One of the aunts pulled out a chair at the long kitchen table that served as a workstation on one end. Another brought her a cup of tea. She breathed in its aroma. A pure, clean, mellow fragrance. Oolong. How did they know?

"You talk. I'll keep making dumplings, Katie," Grandma Dodie said.

"Family favorite," Allie confirmed. "This first night together, we always have Grandma's chicken and dumpling stew."

Twilight's mom pulled her chair and coffee mug closer. "I'm Rhonda. Glad you're here, Katie."

Micah's mom, Deb, gave Katie's shoulders a squeeze before returning to her task of counting out silverware for the evening meal.

"Let's start there," Katie said. But her thoughts wandered for a moment. How did Grandma Dodie spoon dumplings into the massive pot of stew without taking her eyes off Katie? Deep breath. Time to talk. "I need to apologize to all of you. And to Micah when he resurfaces."

Deb's piles of silverware rattled. "For telling him you're not ready to marry him yet?"

"I refused his proposal. If the tables were turned, it would crush me."

"We didn't hear rejection." Rhonda looked at her sisters-in-law for confirmation. Each shook her head. "We heard, 'Not now.'"

Katie's sarcastic gene nudged her. "I'm pretty sure I said no."

"With words, maybe." Deb's coy smile looked so much like one she'd seen on Micah.

"Try the tea," Allie said. "On our Girls' Day in Stillwater tomorrow, we'll stop at the shop where we selected this for you. All kinds of specialty, fair trade spices and teas. Do you like it? It's Green Jade Oolong."

Katie should have majored in psychology. Maybe then she'd know why this family lived in HappyLand all the time instead of once in a while visiting Reality.

"Nobody in this whole family is upset with me for ruining Christmas?"

Allie put her arm around Katie's shoulders. "Sorry, kiddo. You're not that strong. Christmas is going to come, disappointment or not. Do we care about how you must be feeling? Sure we care. Deeply. But we know that's not your whole story."

"Christmas Week with the Binders," Deb said, "is as good a place as they come to figure out where your heart is."

"Mom, do you have any more baby carrots?" Allie stared into the refrigerator, moving things tentatively as if not wanting to disturb the puzzle.

"I'll show you," Deb said.

Of all people, shouldn't Micah's mom have been at least a little peeved that Katie embarrassed her son in front of the people he loved most? Her eyes drifted to the far end of the long kitchen, to the bank of windows facing the backyard. Beside a small, picturesque weathered barn—and what looked like a new addition attached to it—a sloping snow-covered lawn led down to a pond, iced-over. When they'd arrived, sunset's leftover colors painted the snow pink and lavender. It glowed bluish white now. The window seat where she'd spend the next six nights would offer her that view, with the predicted full moon on Christmas Eve.

Nobody used the word *interloper* anymore. And they couldn't call her a squatter if she intended to leave at the end of the week. She wasn't Micah's fiancée. Who was she? And where did she fit in?

Quick answer—nowhere.

"Nice one, Katie." Rhonda's husband, Titus, stood in the kitchen doorway with two thumbs up. Micah stood behind him, clutching the whiteboard. Titus pointed to the board. "Hope you enjoy your"—he read the board—"'All Katie All Day Long' day today. It'll be New Year's Day before your turn in the restroom comes around again. Nice one."

They laughed so effortlessly. Humor had leaked out of the home of her childhood before she'd gotten past the toddler stage. Before she was born, to be more accurate.

"Are you okay?"

Micah's voice would be a dream to wake to every morning. Katie shook herself. Thinking clearly was her strongest asset right now. And she could do it. She was well-rehearsed.

Some were gifted at lip-syncing. She'd learned to stiff-upper-lip sync. "I'm okay."

"Nice comeback with the whiteboard." He took her elbow and steered her toward a mudroom beyond the kitchen.

"Thanks. It was risky. What if they didn't get my sense of humor? The last thing I'd want to do is offend one of them." She kept her voice low. The mudroom wasn't that far from the burgeoning activity in the kitchen.

"Come here, Katie." Micah sat on the low bench near the back door. She joined him. He took her hand and rubbed the spot where the ring would have gone. "I'm not giving up on you. On us. I understand that you need more time. But I thought you should know I'm not giving up."

She wondered if her dad had ever said words like that to her mom. What kind of difference might it have made between them? And for her?

The ring! She tugged her hand away from his and pulled the ring from her pocket. "I haven't had a chance to return this to you. Was it your grandmother's?"

Micah didn't answer right away. "I had it designed to look like hers."

"Well," she said, drawing another breath, "you and your grandfather have good taste." She held the ring out to him.

"I don't want it back."

"I can't keep it. That wouldn't be right."

His shoulders curved forward. "Did you even try it on?"

"Micah."

"I might need to get it sized. For when you do say yes."

Katie leaned against the backrest of the bench. "No one ever accused you of lacking confidence."

"Hopeful. I'm excessively hopeful."

"Your whole blessed family is excessively hopeful, aren't they?"

He leaned back, too, that enchanting coy smile on his face. "You can tell that already?"

"Two minutes in, Micah. Two minutes in."

His hand sluggish and slow, he reached to take the ring from her. "I know what I'll do with it."

Her fingers felt cold now where she'd once grasped that sparkling symbol of Micah's love for her. Love. For her.

He bounced it in the palm of his hand. Two times. Three. On the fourth bounce, it slid from his hand, ricocheted off his knee, and slid under the washing machine directly across from them.

"Micah! What were you thinking?" She jumped to her feet and bent to see if the ring—*Oh, please God!*—had landed within finger reach.

"I didn't plan for that to happen." He dropped to all fours on the floor, the side of his face pressed against the well-worn throw rug.

"You two okay in here?" Micah's dad, Tim. An air of chaperone tone tinged his question.

Katie stood and brushed under-the-washer dust from her hands. "Mr. Binder, he dropped the ring! We need a flashlight and a . . . a yardstick."

"Supper's ready." Grandma Dodie could make herself heard when she wanted to. "Everyone get your hands washed. Then meet up in the kitchen."

Micah's dad shrugged his shoulders. "You heard the woman. Suppertime. We'll tackle that after supper. Make the most of the moment."

"I sense a theme," Katie said, making a mental note to ask Micah—if they were ever truly alone—what made this Christmas likely the last Grandma Dodie and Grandpa Wilson would spend together. She could easily see the effects of an accumulation of years. She wouldn't have had to be a nurse practitioner to observe that. She noted Grandma Dodie's pronounced limp. "Make the most of the moment" was as close as any of them tiptoed to the edge of the conversation. No one seemed interested in talking about the inevitable or how soon it was coming.

Although that might explain why everyone acted so overtly kind. And also why the traffic to the dining tables now slowed as the whole Binder family rushed to look out of the windows facing the backyard to get a glimpse of the moon on snow as it slipped between two pines at the far edge of the pond.

"Look, they're holding hands," one of the granddaughters breathed.

Katie squinted to imagine the pines through the eyes of a child. Lit from behind by a shockingly bright moon. Branches reaching toward each other. Yes, she could see where the girl could get the idea that—

She looked up. The entire family had their eyes trained on Katie and Micah. Holding hands.

Praying before a meal was nothing out of the ordinary for Katie, and even more of a habit since she and Micah started dating. He never forgot the element she'd considered a ritual until Micah showed her the difference between ritual and devotion to the Provider.

He must have learned the art from his father. Timothy Binder's prayer over their relatively simple meal—chicken dumpling stew, homemade applesauce, and crudités Grandma Dodie called a veggie plate—laid a hand of gratitude over it all. And over the family shoe-horned around the tables set up in the family room.

So that's where the term *family room* originated. With a family like the Binders.

The upholstered chairs and couches had been pushed to the perimeter of the room to accommodate two six-foot folding tables and a card table snugged between the Christmas tree and fireplace. They had drawn numbers for seating positions—not to avoid conflict, as would have been the case with Katie's extended family—but to "stir the conversation," as Grandpa Wilson explained it.

"It doesn't matter who you're sitting near," he'd said. "You're going to enjoy it."

She had a feeling that wasn't a command. It was the voice of experience.

To Katie's left sat Micah's mother, Deb. To her right, Madeline, one of the youngest girls. Nine or ten years old. Loose curls that reminded Katie of her own. Directly across the table, Uncle Paul smiled at her, flanked by his brother Titus's older two girls. Twilight, the youngest, danced her way to the card table with her uncle Tim, Grandpa Wilson, and mom, Rhonda—the herbalist who'd named her daughters Twilight, Aurora, and Sunburst.

Katie was going to have to ask which of the young women bookending Paul was Aurora and which was Sunburst. *Micah, I could use your help.* He sat at the head of her table, just out of reach.

"So, how old are you, Madeline?" Katie began after she'd tasted her first spoonful of chicken stew.

"Ten. How old are you?"

Silas, Madeline's dad, caught his daughter's eye and tapped the end of his nose with his index finger. With his eyes bright and head tilted, the action carried no hint of parental threat.

"I'm ten." Madeline smiled at her dad and rubbed her finger on her chin. His brows furrowed, as if he didn't understand her sign language. "Daddy, you have a little something right there," she whispered. Her dad swiped his chin with his napkin and nodded.

Katie dug her spoon into a dumpling. Single dad. Motherless child. They were making it work.

Micah pre-warned her to tread lightly around the subject of Madeline and Mackenzie's mom. Lynda had fought valiantly, Micah said, but the pancreatic cancer had advanced too far before detected. The girls were eight and twelve when they collected their last hugs from her. Katie swallowed the bite of dumpling despite the constriction in her throat. It had nothing to do with carbs.

Uncle Paul crossed his arms on the table and leaned forward, watching Katie eat. He'd been gifted with the perfect face for the comedian and chief practical joker in the family. Much taller and bulkier than Pippin Took in *The Lord of the Rings* movie, his eyes perpetually shone, like Pippin's. His mouth tilted in an ever-present grin.

Katie tried to avoid eye contact. Turned to strike up a conversation with Micah's mom. But Deb was embroiled in a discussion with Aurora, or Sunburst, one of the two, on the subject of piano lesson burnout. Katie crunched a piece of raw cauliflower, chewing all twenty-five recommended times. Uncle Paul didn't discourage easily. She sipped cold cider, swallowed, and sighed as if psyching herself for an exam. "Did you have a question for me?" Katie asked him.

His grin widened. "No question. Watching for that moment when you realize Micah is the best thing that ever happened to you. And you're the best thing that ever happened to him. I don't want to glance away and miss it."

Katie assumed the heat crawling up her neck meant her ears had reddened to the color of the wreath bows on the split-rail fence.

"Paul Stephen Binder! Don't you make me come over there." Grandma Dodie's voice carried above the cacophony.

Paul shrugged and reached for a slice of cheese.

The best thing that happened to Micah? Her? The jury was still out on that verdict. Katie had, after all, humiliated Micah in front of his family. Although every one of them, including Micah, seemed curiously impervious to the sting of humiliation. Their superpower?

"You're good for him," Paul said. "Especially compared to those other—"

"Paul!" Grandma Dodie fired a baby carrot at him from a table away. Dead aim.

"That's my boy," Grandpa Wilson said, clapping his thick-fingered, stiff hands.

Katie leaned back. So, the true Binder family dynamics were about to be unleashed. All that ease with each other, about to erupt into something with which Katie was more familiar. A cavernous spot deep in her core—the part that had started to fill with hope that real families could weather storms and keep loving—caved in. She waited, unbreathing, for harsh words to replace vegetable missiles.

None came. Chatter resumed. Laughter. "Pass the applesauce, please." *Honestly, people. Did Grandma Dodie threaten you all to play nice this week?*

"Katie," Micah's mom said, "Tim and I felt so bad about having to cancel our trip to Florida in August. We so looked forward to meeting you then."

"Glad his surgery turned out okay." Deb pressed her lips together until they almost disappeared. What did that mean?

Katie watched as her maybe-someday-mother-in-law's elegant, long fingers smoothed the sliver of tablecloth between them. She drew a slow breath that moved her chest but not her shoulders.

"Deb?" Should she call her Mrs. Binder? Half the room would answer if she did, and if she were talking louder than barely above mute.

Micah's mother, tastefully blonded hair tucked behind her ears, looked much younger than she probably was. Smooth complexion, as pale as Katie would expect from someone who lived in the Northwoods, sported a faint blush either natural or expertly administered. A woman who somehow pulled off classy and approachable at the same time.

Deb leaned toward Katie. "I hope you and I have some time alone while you're here." She squeezed Katie's hand. The action said more than, "Glad you came."

Katie tried to focus on the stew in front of her, wondering what stews bubbled under the surface of the lives gathered around the dinner tables. Motherless children. Single dad. A couple harboring medical news. A jilted would-be-groom—her own. An engagement ring stuck under the washing machine in the mudroom.

Jilted wasn't the right word. What verb had she committed? She'd said no. Not "I won't," or "I don't want to." Both of those were untrue. Did she mean "I can't"? As in, I can't picture myself as yours forever, Micah? No. That wasn't it. She glanced his way. With his attention focused on his young nieces, Katie could study this enigma of a man from an enigmatic family.

Some might say he looked like a younger, short-cropped version of Bradley Cooper. Same clear blue eyes. Same perpetual smile. Same dusting of whiskers that seemed purposeful rather than unkempt. Katie preferred the Micah version. She watched him lean in toward Sunburst, or Aurora, chuckling at her animated story. He listened with his whole being—eyes, body language, attention, heart.

That.

She'd add that to her Christmas card she'd bought for him. She appreciated the way he dove in to listening like others dive in to a pool. All in.

"Smiling about anything in particular, Katie?"

She dragged her thoughts back to Deb next to her, the mother of the one who'd captured her heart. Katie shrugged. "Life in general?"

"He's a good man, Katie." Deb's words held a lifetime of weight behind them.

"I know." And she did. She stopped herself from blurting, "It's not him. It's me." That sounded cheesier than the way Micah preferred his nachos.

"Wilson, get your fingers off that cookie jar lid."

"Your hearing is still pretty good." Wilson lifted the lid quietly and drew out a peanut butter thumbprint cookie. One. "You're such a fine cook."

"Nice try. But you're the one who made those, while I was working on the cutouts."

"So I did. So I did." He examined the treat for symmetry. Not bad. "You do have more than this one jarful around here somewhere, don't you?"

"All kinds of them."

"Are you going to tell me where?"

"Not on your life."

Wilson watched Dodie's jaw flex as she attempted to keep from smiling. Unsuccessfully. "I love you, old woman."

"You know what they say." She didn't turn from folding towels on the kitchen table.

He took a bite. "Whwht?"

"That a family with an old person in it is in possession of a jewel." She lifted her chin, queen-like. "Chinese proverb."

"Only one old person?" he asked, then popped the rest of the cookie in his mouth and wrapped his arms around her from behind.

She leaned her head against him. "It's better with two."

"I agree," he said, a little jolt shooting through his center.

CHAPTER THREE

"Do your grandparents own a TV?" Katie circled the table, stacking bowls—most of them practically licked clean—while Micah grabbed silverware and dropped it into an ice cream pail of sudsy water.

He chuckled. "What show could possibly be more entertaining than this circus?" He shoved stray carrot missiles into the bowl designated for food scraps.

"Just curious." She stubbed her toe on a chair leg.

"Are you okay?"

About assuming any marriage in which I'm involved is doomed to failure? No. She turned to haul the first stack of bowls to the kitchen sink. "Steel-toed wool socks. Not a problem."

She dodged various Binders engaged in cleanup—anyone whose first name started with *A* through *M*—and grabbed another stack of bowls.

Micah followed and started taking down the folding chairs. "It's in their bedroom closet."

"What is?"

"Their television. Stays buried all week. The Binder men are the only ones in the state of Minnesota who watch all the football games on DVR a week later than the rest of the world. And we don't mind."

Uncle Paul called from the kitchen, "Some of us. Some of us don't mind."

"Those who can stay through New Year's," Micah added, "get the marathon of gridiron action compressed into two days of nonstop football mania, sans commercials. Some of us," he stressed, angling his comment toward the kitchen, "have jobs that won't let us stay that long."

Katie's stomach clenched.

"Which is why I chose teaching for a career path," Paul said. "Yep. The only reason. I don't have to be back to work until after I've caught up on football."

"What are you doing in the kitchen, Uncle Paul? Some teacher. It's not your half of the alphabet serving on the clean-up crew tonight."

"Grandma Dodie needed someone to taste-test the fudge. I told her to get someone else, but she seemed so desperate."

"Paul Stephen Binder!"

"On my way to the barn, Mom."

Micah slipped his arm around Katie's waist. "We'll have to sneak out to the barn later too."

Katie elbowed his middle.

He drew back, his hand over his heart. "Good lady, I know not what thou must have been thinking. I referreth to yonder barn addition tack room, which now serveth as . . . well . . . as a tack room"—he lost his Old English accent—"and rec center, and is the warming house for those who skate, snowshoe, cross country ski . . ."

"I'm a Floridian. Native."

"Snowshoeing is a lot like walking in scuba flippers in deep sand. You'll catch on fast."

"Or break a major bone."

"Which shouldn't be a problem with your medical knowledge. Nurse practitioners can set their own bones, can't they?" he teased. "When I told the family you were coming for the week, I billed you as our circus nurse. You're okay with that, right?" He kissed her on her forehead.

Was preserving the sanctity of the Binder Family Christmas Week reason enough to postpone telling him what was coming? If this kind of family was what he was looking for, she was the unlikeliest candidate for a wife. Could she beg for a little peace on earth on that subject until after Christmas Day at least? It was time she was honest about their future together. But not right now.

"Here, Dad. I'll get that." Tim, Micah's father, took the folding chair from Wilson Binder. "Plenty of us around to help. No need to stress your heart any more than necessary."

Grandpa Binder's heart. Her suspicions were right. All the more reason why now was not the right time.

"I'm not done living yet, son."

"Which is why"—Tim grunted as he hoisted the banquet

table onto its side and collapsed its legs—"you should take advantage of all this muscle power while you have it around this week."

Tim. Starts with a *T*. The man was as thoughtful as his son. His section of the alphabet wasn't serving. It didn't seem to matter. Katie smiled. Paul, Silas, Timothy, Titus. Dodie and Wilson hadn't given birth to any sons who naturally fell into Cleanup Crew One.

Wilson found his favorite armchair, still among those lined up around the perimeter of the room as if framing a dance floor, and lowered himself into it. "You won't catch me arguing with that logic. I don't mind relinquishing my role as the only muscles around here for a few days."

"Is the neighbor boy still coming over to help with Jericho?" Tim asked.

Another family member she had yet to meet?

"Horse," Micah mouthed. Who had she known who so deftly anticipated her needs?

"The boy and his folks took off for parts unknown this week," Grandpa answered. "Disney Cruise or something. Miss him." Grandpa Binder rubbed his left shoulder. Katie tried to mask her concern as she cleared the rest of the meal remnants while she observed him.

Micah and his dad reset the family room while the *A* through *M* women loaded the dishwasher, put away the left-overs, cleaned the counters, and chatted about their girl's day out the following day.

Katie's true confession could wait. It wouldn't change anything except make it clearer why Micah would have regretted it if Katie had accepted his proposal.

Grandma Dodie and Deb prepped two batches of baked French toast for the morning and gentled them into the already full refrigerator.

"Want me to take the cider to the fridge in the tack room?" Paul's wife, Allie, asked. "That'll free up a little space."

"Good idea. I'd suggest we nestle it in a snowbank, but the Stanleys next door said we have a bear who is resisting hibernation like a toddler resists an afternoon nap. You girls be careful," Grandma Dodie said, "if you're out walking alone. I don't recommend it. Walking"—her voice seemed to drift to another plane of thought—"alone. Not . . . recommended."

Allie put her arm around her mother-in-law. Dodie leaned her head on Allie's shoulder.

It never lifted, despite the humor and tender moments. It remained like an unfortunate stain on an otherwise tidings-of-great-joy holiday—the ever-present threat that this was the last year they'd spend together as an intact family. Katie would survive her personal crisis. Micah was the kind of guy who would rebound. Neither of their concerns was worth wasting worry over compared to what this older couple faced.

Katie determined to do all she could to push aside the constriction around her heart, to put her distress on hold and help this family milk all the love they could from this last holiday with Grandpa Wilson. It was the least she could do.

The Christmas music looped around to the familiar song about being home for Christmas. She prayed Grandpa Wilson's heart would hold out long enough to allow the family sweet memories in this place that defined the essence of home.

Katie rubbed her upper arms, chilled by the clear picture of what she'd missed.

"Too cold for a moonlit walk?" a familiar voice spoke near her ear.

"What's the temp outside?" she asked.

Micah came around to face her. "If you have to ask, it's too cold. I know, native Floridians have to be broken in slowly to these conditions. We can wait for another night."

Katie glanced at the Binder women who'd stopped what they were doing to hear her response. "Grandma Dodie says there's a bear who—"

"Won't be a problem," Micah said, patting his hip.

"You have a gun? You didn't tell me you carry a gun."

Micah's laughter mingled with that of the Binder women. "Not a gun, Katie. Fudge. We'll throw fudge at him and run like crazy."

"Won't the smell of fudge attract a bear?" She'd watched a few Alaska survivor shows.

"Good point," he said. "You carry it." He reached into his pocket and pulled out a small canister.

"That's pepper spray."

"So it is. I guess we'll have to rely on that." Micah's eyes glinted. "Want me to grab your coat for you?"

"You know which one it is among all those?"

"I can tell by the smell."

"Micah!"

"Bad word. Bad word. I mean, by the fragrance."

Katie planted her hands on her hips. "I bought it at Goodwill. I don't own a winter coat, as you can imagine. So I bought it secondhand."

"Not that fragrance." Micah lifted his hands in surrender. "Try to say something romantic and look what you get."

"My counsel, Micah?" His mom snatched up the last of the dishtowels and headed for the mudroom. "Quit taking relationship advice from your uncle Paul. No offense, Allie."

"Oh, none taken. I'm married to the guy. I would have said it if you hadn't." The sisters-in-law high-fived each other.

The delight of a functional family that seemed to find humor in the smallest things washed over her. "Poor Micah. It's hard being the only male grandchild sometimes, isn't it? My coat is the—"

"You don't have to tell me. I really do know."

He brought her the right coat. Someone else's scarf and hat.

"Micah, these aren't—"

"Aren't yours. I know. Yours were stylin'. Don't get me wrong. But a little wimpy for walking in these temps. I borrowed them from Elisa."

"Elisa?" She'd never get these names straight.

"Paul's oldest."

"But Micah, *stylin'?*" She scrunched her nose.

He shrugged into his coat. “Be right with you.” He gave his grandmother a hug and told her he loved her. Did the same with his mom when she reentered the kitchen from the mudroom.

“We’re just going for a walk, right?” Katie pulled on her gloves and slid into her boots. “We’re not risking our lives out there, are we?” She felt in her coat pocket for the pepper spray.

“I always tell the women in my life—including you, if you hadn’t noticed—that I love them before I walk out the door.” Micah held the door for her. They stepped out into the crystal bright night. “Habit, I guess.”

“Because you never know when it will be the last opportunity?”

“One of these days, it will be.” He would have sounded matter-of-fact if not for the faint catch in his voice. “Watch your step here. The stones on the path heave with the cold.”

A few fat flakes danced in the bluish light of moon on snow. A yard light attached to the compact barn spread its competing illumination in a wide arc. With the moon that bright, Katie almost asked if they could douse the yard light. Where were the flakes coming from? The moon seemed unimpeded by clouds. Maybe it, too, picked its path carefully.

She slipped her hand into the crook of Micah’s elbow for stability. Emotional as well as physical. They hadn’t had any extended time alone since they’d arrived, since she refused his ring . . . which was still hiding under the washing machine! “Micah! The ring . . .”

"About that. I apologize." He steered them toward the long driveway. "I should have realized meeting my family would be more than enough stress without adding a major life decision like that into the first few minutes."

"They've been wonderful."

"I'm quite fond of them." He kicked at the fresh inch of fluff at their feet.

"Do I need any prep work for my time with The Girls tomorrow?"

"And by that you mean . . . ?"

"I don't know what's expected of me."

"Enjoy yourself." He said it as if she should have known.

She stopped walking. "You do know," she said, "that those people in there aren't normal. Forgiveness is second nature to them. Nobody holds a grudge. The in-laws are indistinguishable from the children born into the family."

"Except the in-laws are all girls."

"You know what I mean. Don't they ever mess up? Get mad at each other? Throw a fit? Lose their temper? Be petty with one another?"

"You've only been here a few hours. Give it time."

"I have a feeling a Binder hissy-fit doesn't look anything like the ones I've seen my parents—and most of the world, for that matter—lob at each other."

Micah snugged her borrowed hat over her ears then rested his hands on her shoulders. "What if . . . ?"

She waited. Counted snowflakes and Micah's blinks. "Go on."

"What if this kind of crazy love is normal and everything else is the warped way of living?"

"An entire family of sanguine personalities?"

He shook his head. "So much deeper than that. Come on. I want to show you something."

He took her hand and pulled her off the driveway into the deeper snow. Birch trees shone blue-white against the backdrop of taller and fuller pines. She had to admit that moon on snow rivaled moon on the Gulf. They followed the faint shadow that marked a path not shoveled but carved by foot traffic.

Their breaths came in visible puffs in the cold air. They breathed in rhythm, but not on the same beat. She supposed some would take that as a sign of a doomed relationship. She shook off the idea, temporarily.

"Too cold?"

Had she really shaken? And yes. She'd been accused of being too cold. She came by it naturally. From a long line of the familially inept. One would think a person with a poisoned family line wouldn't be obsessed as she was with connecting her ancestral dots.

"Katie? I asked if you were too cold." He snugged his arm around her.

"Not now."

"We have to go single file up ahead."

"We're going into the woods? In the dark?" That was a genuine shiver.

"It's not far."

She grabbed the back of his jacket as he led the way. "If this is some kind of Binder family initiation ritual . . ."

"Kind of," he said.

His jovial tone didn't help quell her concern. Woods plus dark equaled danger in every fairy tale she knew.

A trail of sorts cut through the woods at an angle away from the house and yard. Moonlight peeked between the trees, but couldn't maintain a steady light source for them.

"Micah, you have a flashlight with you, I assume?"

"We won't need it."

"You might not."

He reached around to grab her hand and pull her deeper into the woods. "Yes, I have a flashlight." The trail took another turn, departing from the main path. "With batteries?"

"Katie."

"Confirming." The soles of her boots squeaked the snow. "Humor me?"

"Always. If you'll give me the chance."

Her sigh made a cloud of vapor in the night air. "How much longer?"

"Forever. That's what always means." He kept tugging her toward the unspoken destination, his heart's message audible in his words.

"I mean, how much farther are we walking?"

He stopped abruptly. She stubbed the toe of her boot on the back of his. Micah stepped to the side and let her see what made him halt. They stood in a small clearing on a cliff high above the St. Croix River. He edged closer. The captivating sight urged her forward, but the unpredictability of the snow at her feet kept her well back from the edge.

He hugged a tree so near the cliff, its roots showed like a can-can dancer's legs.

"Micah, be careful."

"This is one of my favorite views of the river."

"Beautiful." She pressed her back against the rough trunk of a tree on the woods side of the overlook. "I can see why it's a favorite. I wish I had my phone. The light from the moon might not be enough to capture an image, though."

"That's why we stay until we have it memorized."

She followed his line of sight to the curve of Wisconsin on the far side, to flickers of light from other homes, other families. The only snow falling now came from tree branches when the barely-there wind brushed past them.

His breath puffs sailed out across the expanse. Slow, measured, as if even his heart rate and respiration responded to the still scene.

"How do you do that?" she asked, tucking her gloved hands into her coat pockets.

"Do what?"

"Just be. Here. In the moment. Fully present. As if there aren't twenty people crammed into that small house back there somewhere"—she nodded down the trail they'd taken—"and your job isn't making you insane, and we didn't have a super-awkward moment a couple of hours ago, and there's no such thing as . . . as . . ."

"Death and taxes?" He didn't take his gaze from the frozen river.

So, he had been thinking about his grandfather.

"Moments like this," he said, "might never have the opportunity for a replay."

"This might be the last?" Somehow when Micah or the other members of his family said it, the phrase didn't sound morbid. "You unplug far more successfully than I do."

He left his tree and crossed to where she leaned. "It's a learned skill."

"I need lessons."

"Step away from the tree." He stood behind her. Close. So close. "Hold your arms out like airplane wings." He did the same, cupped her hands in his, and wrapped both his and her arms around her. "Now lean your head against my chest. Good. Look out beyond where we are. Breathe with me."

She noticed more stars than she'd seen earlier. And faint sounds. The rustle of dry leaves still clinging ferociously to a lone branch despite being long past the season for falling. The crackle of ice shifting. The soul-filling smell of wood smoke.

Micah's laundry soap. And air crisped by fresh snow and invigorating cold.

A dog barked far in the distance. Lights across the river flickered and went out. Others flicked on. Life. Preparing for Christmas. Life. In his arms.

Forever sounded wonderful at that pace.

CHAPTER FOUR

"This isn't the way we came." Katie focused on stepping into the depressions Micah had made with his previous steps. No trail here.

"It'll get us home. Shortcut."

"About time for that flashlight, isn't it?" She could feel snow crusting on the legs of her jeans. All with which they had to navigate now was an eerie glow that almost seemed to rise from the snow cover. The pines blocked all but a few stray moonbeams. The spindly trees were kinder. "I mean, I'm all for adventure, but . . ."

"Look over my shoulder," Micah said.

"What?"

He angled sideways and extended his hand like a maître d' in a five-star restaurant. "Voilà! Home."

Viewed from this direction, the time-weathered barn blocked most of the benefits of the yard light, but Katie could see its outline and knew warmth wasn't far. Her toes and nose needed a warm-up. Maybe her insides too.

The word *home* fell so gently from Micah's lips. Had Katie ever known a time when others would have said the same of her? No, not even when she was in elementary school. Her mother and father made their disgust for one another easy enough for a child to understand. Her paternal grandparents lived too far away. Katie's maternal grandparents, too close. Their dysfunctions played out at the end of the block, too often in the yard and loud enough to reach Katie's house and keep her from inviting friends over.

What was their problem?

She knew. And now it was her problem. Hers and Micah's.

"So," Micah said as they drew close to the back door of his grandparents' cottage, "ice skating tomorrow?" He kissed her frozen nose.

Pull it together, Katie. He—and his family—deserve a Christmas without drama. Her parents may not have managed it since their first holiday as husband and wife, but she could find a way to cope with unbridled joy for a week. Couldn't she?

"So sorry to disappoint you, Micah. But tomorrow is"—she whipped off her borrowed hat and fluffed her hair—"Girls' Day. Remember?"

He held the door for her. "Ohhhh. Guess we'll have to find some skates that fit you and get right out there now, huh?"

"Hot cider. Hot cocoa. Coffee. Tea. Something along those lines. All I want right now."

Their flight had left Fort Myers early that morning. How long before the household settled down tonight so she could make her nest there in the window seat? No shades on the long bank of windows. She'd be awake with the sunrise. Or with the first person who needed to brew a cup of coffee.

"Hot cider's my preference. Want me to make one for each of us?" Micah asked.

"Thanks. I'm going to"—she searched for a more delicate wording—"see if the bathroom's free at the moment."

It wasn't. She was third in line. Interesting conversations, though, in the hallway.

"Anyone more desperate than I am?" the first in line—Deb—asked when the current occupant vacated the room.

Katie joined Uncle Paul and Aunt Allie's youngest—Bella—waving Deb into the room.

While they waited, Bella, eighteen, whispered, "How are you handling the no technology rule?"

"Managing," Katie answered. "You?"

Bella said, "Other than the thumb-twitching? Better this year than the last couple. If you'd been here last year, you would have seen a theater-quality pout."

"How did your folks respond to that?"

"Ignored my silent tantrum for a while. After two days of it, they made me take it outside. Yeah, talk about mature. I acted that way the year before too. Same results. Go figure." She poked a finger into her forehead as if willing her brain to apologize for previous behavior.

Katie smiled. "So far so good this year?"

"It's tougher than ever. I miss Jeffrey."

"Your boyfriend?" Bella's head tilt told Katie she'd guessed wrong. "My dog," Bella said.

"You miss texting with your dog?"

"He stays with my bestie when I'm gone. We Skype. It keeps him from having a meltdown."

"Your bestie?"

"No. Jeffrey." Little hint of irritation in her voice.

The bathroom door opened. Bella slipped in as Deb slipped out. Katie heard the door lock click, and then heard the sound of water running in the shower. No!

Katie felt her facial muscles strain as her eyes widened. Now what?

The door clicked open. Bella stuck her head out. "Kidding. I'm not showering. It'll be your turn in a sec." She winked. "I am my father's daughter."

What would it be like to make a statement like that with pride coloring the words? Katie could be proud, and always would be, of her father's accomplishments in engineering. Such a gift for inventing. Heart connections, on the other hand, made no sense to him.

And her mom? Didn't they have anger management classes when her mom was a child? A new wife? A young mom? Katie hadn't lived through the first two phases, but she well knew what a mom's penchant for anger could look like every day since.

Only rarely directed at Katie, it still fouled the air of their home, stained every conversation, kept her mom mired in a mood just shy of paranoia. The grocery bagger didn't just forget to double-bag the ice cream. He disrespected her. The mail delivery person wasn't a few minutes late. He intentionally tried to make Katie's mom miserable. Her husband's lack of attention became two weeks of icy silence punctuated with huffs and sighs.

When Katie turned twelve, they divorced. They must have thought she could handle it by then. Her mother won custody by default. Her father didn't know how to raise a preteen girl, nor did he have any interest in learning. Katie was too complicated an engineering project, apparently.

Even before Katie started reading her Bible and going to church with a friend from school, her child-sized heart knew there was a better way to approach life and its disappointments. She knew it.

She'd found it, understood it, embraced it in her late teens. College gave her a reprieve from the tensions at home with a perpetually persecuted parent. Adulthood made Katie sensitive to avoid those with anger issues like her mom's, which trimmed her circle of friends and acquaintances to a bare minimum.

Then Micah. Nothing rattled him except the things that should. Injustice. Unkindness. Cruelty. And the occasional bad call by a referee.

Was it any wonder his attention made her feel like she was finally popping to the surface after holding her breath under water too long?

The bathroom door snapped open. Bella floated out and bowed to signify it was Katie's turn. Katie's turn . . . to let go of what she couldn't correct in her family history? The text she'd gotten on the way to Stillwater had stolen her last hope that someone from her lineage had done marriage well. She closed the bathroom door behind her and leaned against it. Who was she kidding?

Micah stood leaning against the opposite wall when she emerged. He held a mug in each hand. She reached for the one he extended toward her.

"I reheated it for you," he said.

"Sorry. There was a line."

His grin warmed her more than the hot mug in her hands. "There's almost always a line. Did anyone tell you we have a second bathroom out in the barn?"

"Oh, that sounds appealing."

"It's not what you're thinking. We call the whole thing 'the barn' even though only a third of it is for Jericho."

She held the mug to her chest, letting the steam warm her chin and nose. "When will I meet Jericho?"

"Tomorrow. The garage, the rec center addition, and the stall for Jericho and loft for hay. Sure you don't want to stay home with us guys tomorrow and go exploring?"

"Don't listen to him," Deb said, heading to the bathroom with a stack of clean towels. "He's had ten months to get to know you. It's our turn now." The expression she wore read as genuine as the hand-pressed cider. And at least as sweet.

Micah acquiesced and steered Katie toward the family room where various Binders huddled on opposite sides of the room.

"We get Katie!" a voice called out.

"No fair. Micah can't draw to save his soul." The opposing team made its voice heard.

Micah huffed, hands on hips. "I'll have you know I've been practicing my stick figures." He joined the team that protested, wedging himself onto an already full couch. He drew wildly in the air.

Katie took the folding chair she was offered and set her cider on the low table behind it. "How do you know I can draw? Pictionary, right?"

"Right," Rhonda said. "Despite our façade of competitiveness, the mess-ups are the fun part. They keep the game interesting."

"You'll do great," the youngest, Twilight, added. "This round is movie titles."

"Since kindergarten, I've been an only child," Katie said. "So we didn't play a lot of games at home." That, and a few other reasons. She'd let the "since kindergarten" slip without thinking. Game strategizing noise adequately covered what she'd said, except for Rhonda and Twilight, whose quizzical looks she'd have to answer eventually.

"You're up," Micah said from across the room.

"Me? First?" She looked at her teammates. "Is that such a good idea?"

"Tradition," Twilight said. "We always make Micah's girlfriends go first." She handed Katie the dry erase marker and pointed her to the whiteboard propped on an empty chair.

Titus wasn't the only one who caught his daughter's faux pas. He tapped the tip of his nose. Twilight didn't notice. Micah did. He flushed from ruggedly handsome Florida tan to a color not unlike the cranberries strung on the tree.

Katie uncapped the marker. All the girlfriends, huh? No wonder the Binders had forgiven her so quickly. It had happened before? *How many times has that ring hung on the tree, Micah?* The ring. Someone had retrieved it from under the washing machine, right? She pulled her movie title from the stack of cards in the Pictionary box.

Seriously?

She looked heavenward, not for inspiration, but sympathy. Not funny. At all. How was she supposed to draw a picture that would make her team guess the movie *The Proposal*?

Focus, Katie. She twirled the marker. *All the girlfriends Micah brings home.*

"Time starts . . . now!" a male voice said.

The cold air from their walk through the woods made her eyes water. She brushed at what had collected in the corners and pressed the tip of the marker against the board. She drew a circle with a blob at the top and lines radiating from the blob.

"Breakfast at Tiffany's!"

"Lord of the Rings!"

She shook her head and drew a stick figure with long hair and another stick figure facing the first. Then she drew a line from the kneeling figure to the ring to the woman . . . and back to the man.

"The Proposal!" Micah shouted.

"Hey, you're not on our team!"

Katie capped the marker and tossed it to the opposing side. "But he apparently knows a lot about proposals." She sauntered back to her folding chair.

A chorus of "ooh's" followed her.

"Extra points for Katie."

"One proposal. One!" Micah said. "All the others were . . ."

All the others.

Rhonda stood in front of her, facing outward, like a bodyguard, arms out and down in protective mode. "Let's keep the game moving, okay? We can't stay up too late tonight. Big day tomorrow. Aurora, is it your turn?"

"No. It's Micah's turn."

Rhonda turned to face Katie. "You go ahead, Aurora. Micah's currently in time-out."

The house quieted in layers. Cheers from the winning team faded as each family unit clustered, completed their pre-bedtime routines, and prepared to settle into spare bedrooms, odd corners of the family room, or don their coats and boots to head for the barn's tack/rec room addition Katie had yet to see.

Each Binder filed past Grandma Dodie and Grandpa Wilson for hugs and "I love you" good nights. Grandpa whispered something in each one's ear. Katie watched, unsure of the protocol for a non-family member. In unison, the two leaders of the Binder family motioned her closer to their side-by-side chairs.

"Good night, sweet Katie," Grandma Dodie said and kissed her on the cheek. "You are so deeply loved."

Katie almost pulled back, primed to respond, *What have I done to make you love me? Or is that what you say to "all the girlfriends" Micah brings home for Christmas?*

Grandpa Wilson feigned impatience for his turn. He hugged Katie with a strength that surprised her. The nurse practitioner in her listened to his breath sounds and heartbeat while he held her. He whispered in her ear as he had with his own family members.

"Lord God, guard us through the night and wake us already loving You more. In the Name of Jesus, the unending Light in our darkness, amen."

When he finally released her from the hug, Katie stood with a vow filling her chest. If she ever had children, she would bless them every night with a prayer like that. Including as often as she could after they were grown and gone. And she would pronounce the "a-" part of amen as he had. Ah. Or was it awe?

Grandpa Wilson gripped her hand in his as if expecting her to stay beside him while Micah—the last Binder to be blessed—stepped forward. Only the rudest of women would wrench free from that grip because of the unspoken tension hanging like low-lying wood smoke between them.

Micah kissed his grandmother on the cheek and told her he loved her. She did the same, then took his face in her hands and drew him closer until their noses touched. Clear dark brown eyes inches away from clear blue eyes. Dodie's eyes communicated something Micah seemed to understand. When he pulled back, he nodded and smiled. She nodded only once, as if punctuating what she'd "said."

The look he gave Katie as he moved toward his grandfather broke her heart. It wasn't the typical "I'm in trouble, aren't I?" apology. She didn't have long enough to study his expression before Micah bent to hug his grandfather.

"Love you, Grandpa. Always."

"I love you, too, Micah. Always."

The whispered prayer in Micah's ear seemed longer than the one he'd prayed over Katie. Micah stood, brushing at his eyes.

No wonder Micah would have moved heaven and earth to be here for this.

"So, you two will talk in the morning, right?" Grandpa Wilson made a pronouncement rather than a request.

Grandma Dodie added, "We're not staying up until you get this worked out. We need our wisdom sleep." She winked at Katie. "We gave up calling it beauty sleep—what?—two decades ago, Wilson?"

"About that." He released Katie's hand and reached for his wife's. "And yet, you seem more beautiful to me every day. How do you pull that off, my bride?"

Micah helped Grandma Dodie out of her chair. "Sixty watt bulbs," she said. "They don't reveal as much as the seventy-fives. I'm on the hunt for forties, if I can find them. Maybe in pink."

Grandpa Wilson let Katie hold his elbow while he rose from his chair. "Did anyone tell you, Katie, that you look a lot like a grown-up, healthy version of that sweet-faced child in the *Les Miserábles* movie?"

"My theater teacher in high school thought so," Katie said. "Guess which role I snagged. Then she discovered acting isn't my gift." Although she was doing a pretty good job acting as if Christmas Week at the Binders wasn't challenging everything in her. "Good night, everyone."

Grateful she had a room of her own, even though it was the kitchen, Katie worked on creating her nest on the cushioned window seat. Someone had already lined the bottom third of the window with a quilt draft-stopper. She grabbed the pillow and bedding from the storage area under the window seat. Among the bedding was a handwritten note and two thermal heating pads. "Heat these in the microwave for two minutes. One for your feet. The other to hug."

A few minutes later, she crawled into her narrow bed, her feet toasty warm. She hugged the other heated square to her chest and watched the night sky visible above the quilt barrier. With the quilt propped that way, she couldn't see the yard light, only the stars through the paned window. Stars relentless in their faithfulness. Predictable. Trustworthy. Enduring. The same stars that dotted the sky over Bethlehem millennia ago.

She'd traced her family line back prior to the Civil War and not found a hint of that kind of faithfulness or predictability. But she'd seen strong glimpses of it here, in this house, in less than a day.

Tomorrow, would it all disintegrate? Would the press of people fuel tempers and ignite the kind of holiday drama that had been the Vale family tradition? The Binders couldn't keep up this "Behave yourselves. We have company" aura the whole week, could they?

Micah had. For ten months. He'd maintained his even-tempered, overtly kind attitude. Had she been waiting for it to crumble? Expecting him to arrive one day without his mask in place?

All the girlfriends.

That was it. He'd been practicing.

She knew he'd dated others. So had she. But he'd failed to mention the parade of women he'd dragged to the cottage for the holidays with his family. How many women's fingers had that ring fit?

The ring. She should get out of her nest and check for it under the washer. Should.

The still house heard one last song. Not a Christmas song at all. Grandpa Wilson must have been standing in the hallway outside the master bedroom in order for it to carry all the way to where she lay. His well-worn voice sang:

The Lord has promised good to me,
His Word my hope secures;
He will my Shield and Portion be,
As long as life endures.

That was all. One stanza only of John Newton's "Amazing Grace." Was he losing touch with reality? Was that all he could remember? And why that song a few days before Christmas? Curious man. She tugged the embrace of his prayer for her tighter than the quilt, but felt the cold draft of "as long as life endures."

"Dodie? Are you okay?"

His wife rolled toward him in the bed they'd shared for more than six decades. "Can't get comfortable tonight," she said.

"Your hip?"

"Among other things."

He could see little more than her shadow in the dim light from the small lamp in the master bath. Her shadow. Familiar. Constant. More than he deserved. He reached to brush back the silver curls that always drifted over her forehead when she lay on her side. They had. Softer than when they'd been the color of a freshly milled walnut plank and her waist had just fit between his hands. "That Katie. Do you think she was overwhelmed by all of us watching, or do you think she really doesn't want to marry our Micah?"

"Marriage is not an institution that should be entered into lightly, Wilson."

A lifetime of meaning threaded its way through her words. "I give the girl credit. It would have been easy for her to go along with it for now, what with Christmas, and the family, and the love she can't hide."

"You saw it, too, didn't you?" She slid closer and rested her head on his chest.

"I recognize real love better than I used to," he said.

The one tear he felt drop from the corner of her eye to his chest would be the only one, he knew. And he wasn't surprised it had fallen.

"She's still sleeping."

"No, she isn't. I saw her eyeballs move."

"You can't see her eyeballs, Twilight. They're under her eyelids."

"Did too. Saw them moving under her eyelids."

"People do that when they dream, you know."

Katie opened one eye.

"Told you. Awake."

"She is now," Grandma Dodie said. "With all that chirping going on. Good morning, Katie."

Katie tugged the covers to her neck and sat up. "What time is it?" Her morning eyes couldn't see as far as the clock on the microwave. What she could see was the five girl cousins, fourteen and under, seated at the kitchen table a few feet away. They all wore knit hats. Handknit, it looked like. Red with their names in white lettering circling the turned-up ribbing.

"Good morning, Madeline, Mackenzie, Sunburst, Aurora, Twilight." They hadn't switched hats to throw her off, had they? No one flinched or giggled. "And good morning, Grandma Dodie."

"The girls are having their baked French toast already, since Silas is taking them to Taylors Falls today while we older women head into Stillwater. We'll be a large enough crew to navigate through the holiday crowds."

Katie tucked the covers around her back and dug with her toes for the no-longer-warm thermal pad at her feet. "Silas is taking this whole group?"

Madeline piped up. "My mom's sister lives in Taylors Falls. Aunt Gloria has an indoor pool at her house because of our cousin Liz's legs."

Older sister Mackenzie rolled her eyes at Madeline. "Liz has muscular dystrophy."

"That's when—"

"She knows what that means, Maddie. She's a nurse."

Grandma Dodie set a bowl of fruit in the middle of the table. "Girls."

Sunburst adjusted her hat. "So, we get to go along and swim all day when those two visit their aunt Gloria at Christmas. Merry Christmas to us!"

Katie felt a wave of emotion for what it must be like for Silas to raise his two girls alone. No small challenge.

"If you're talking that loud, Katie must be awake," Silas said as he entered the kitchen and kissed Dodie on the cheek. "Love you, Mom."

"You too, son."

"Are you girls almost ready?" Silas poured a cup of coffee.

"Daddy, Grandma made us use plastic forks so we wouldn't wake Katie."

"Your grandmother is a very wise woman."

"Plastic!" Aurora said. "Don't tell my mom, Uncle Silas. She's all-organic, you know."

"Except for Christmas Week," Rhonda said, joining the circus in the kitchen.

Katie adjusted the bedcovers like a buffalo robe, grabbed clean clothes from her carry-on under the window seat, and scooted past the rapidly forming crowd. "Must. Brush. Teeth," she explained, her lips barely moving.

How had she slept through coffee brewing, the oven door opening and closing, the aromas that she now knew penetrated the whole house, and five girls eating breakfast? Not falling asleep until after two in the morning might have contributed.

The bathroom door opened just as she reached it. Micah. He looked like she felt.

"Good morning, Katie." He held her by her blanket-padded shoulders and kissed her cheek. He smelled like winter sunshine. She, on the other hand . . .

She held her hand over her mouth. "Teeth. Morning breath. Gotta go." She ducked into the bathroom and emerged less than ten minutes later, clean, dressed, hair and makeup yet undone.

Micah stood where she'd left him. "How'd you sleep?"

She shrugged.

"Me too. For the record," he said, "I've only proposed to one woman in my life. You. The others were . . ."

The small hairs on the back of her neck fought with each other.

"Let me rephrase that. I've had other girlfriends."

"I knew that."

"And I invited a couple of them here for Christmas." Micah's gaze held hers.

"How many is a couple?"

"Counting high school? Three."

Did Katie want to ask the next, obvious question? "What happened to those relationships?"

"They're gone."

Katie fingered her hair off her forehead. "I'm glad to hear that. What I meant was, how did they end? Why?" She had an ancestry file that could have given him a few options.

He sighed. "I didn't know what I was looking for then. I do now."

"And what have you been looking for?"

He stepped closer. She took a half-step back. "A love that will last. Like my parents' and grandparents'."

She would have doubled over if he hadn't been standing too close. Her greatest fear hung suspended between them. He wanted forever. "I hope you enjoy your search then, Micah. I can't be that person."

Against her norm, she dove into the crowd this time, making conversation with the Binder women now gathered in the kitchen for their round at the table.

"Are you okay, Katie?" Deb asked, handing her a cup of coffee.

She sniffed. "Soap in my eye. And no makeup. And I can't find my curling iron. That explains the—" She circled her face with her hand.

"Micah, shoo!" Deb said. "Girls Day has officially started. You can have her back close to suppertime. Scoot! Your dad and grandpa and uncle Paul are waiting for you in the garage. They have a project. We'll save breakfast for you."

Have her back. Katie couldn't tell them it was no longer an issue. What Micah wanted, she could never provide.

"You should never use soap near your eyes, Katie." Rhonda moved a chair out for her. "And coconut oil is much better for your skin in general."

"Look at that complexion," Allie said. "Does it look like it's suffering from soap damage, Rhonda?"

"Or tea tree oil." Undaunted, Rhonda listed her favorite all-natural products while Katie stabbed at the luxurious, custardy French toast with maple syrup on the plate in front of her. She looked up once. Micah no longer stood in the doorway.

What were the odds he'd be willing to give up part of the day tomorrow to drive her to the airport? No. She'd never get a flight this close to Christmas.

Wilson didn't like that Dodie's limp seemed more pronounced since the kids arrived. Maybe she moved at a quicker pace with them there. Lots to do. She'd always thrived on that. Neither one of thcm moved as they once did.

He lowered the footrest on his recliner. Micah snatched his coat from the pegs near the door. "Where you going, number-one grandson?"

"One and only, Grandpa. I'm heading out to feed Jericho. If that's okay."

"I was on my way. But if you've got your heart set on it, I believe I'll let you do that today."

Micah pulled on his gloves. "You okay, Grandpa?"

"Always better when the family's here."

"We're not too much for you?"

Wilson gave Micah the best scowl he could muster.

"Okay, okay." The boy stopped with his hand on the doorknob. "You want to do a little ice fishing later?"

Truth be told, no. "We'll have to see. I haven't been out on the ice yet this year."

"With that stretch of bitter cold I heard you guys had up here late November, early December, the ice is sure to be thick enough. I might dig a test hole to see."

"More power to you." *These days I don't have the strength to dig a hole in my mashed potatoes.*

CHAPTER FIVE

WITH EVERY STROKE OF HER mascara wand, Katie steeled herself for the day ahead. "Enjoying" Stillwater would take considerable fortitude, in light of the pending talk that would seal her relationship with Micah as a thing of the past.

She'd set aside grave disappointment before in order to function in public, in her job, even at church, with her friends. One day. She could manage one day of whatever it took to keep the mood light with these unique women. Grandma Dodie deserved a day of joy. They all did.

Katie started packing, mentally, then stopped herself. The Binders squeezed every drop of delight from life by staying present in the moment. It was a good day for Katie to practice the art. She swiped gloss across her lips and smiled into the mirror. She heard her drama club instructor in her ear: *Let them see your smile and hear your sigh from the back row.* The sigh would be easier to pull off than a natural smile.

All seven women, counting the two college students—Bella and Elisa—squeezed into Rhonda's van. Grandma Dodie called shotgun, as if anyone else would have dared usurp her right to ride in front. Katie found a place next to Allie on the second seat. Deb, Bella, and Elisa crammed themselves into the back.

They'd only gotten through two Christmas carols on the radio—three-part harmony, nice—before Rhonda slowed the van as they wove their way through Stillwater, each woman spotlighting a "can't miss" point of interest she thought Katie might appreciate. Had it been only yesterday afternoon when she and Micah had passed these same buildings?

"First stop," Grandma Dodie said, "Darn. Knit. Anyway."

"What?" Katie wondered what she'd missed.

"The knitting shop," Allie said. "Darn. Knit. Anyway. Cutest place. Grandma Dodie's friends plus the occasional traveling knitter sit, knit, and chat on the upper level where the couches are."

"And crochet," Grandma Dodie added from the front seat. "I'm using my Christmas money from Wilson to stock up on yarn for the winter. Could be a long one."

They pulled into a slushy parking area on the east side of Main Street at the end of Stillwater. Rhonda helped her mother-in-law out of the van and into the building.

"Watch this," Deb said. "Rhonda will come back and tell us Grandma said, 'Don't forget to pick me up in time for lunch.' Same routine every year. As if we could ever leave her out. Do you like antiquing, Katie?"

These women wouldn't know why a question about shopping or spending twisted her insides. "Small apartment. So my antique hunting is usually limited to old books or jewelry."

"Like . . . rings?" Elisa said.

Allie turned in her seat. Katie caught the warning in the look Allie directed at her daughter.

"We know a couple of great shops for old books and jewelry," Deb said. "The Staples Mill has three levels of antiques, thirty-three dealers. You'll get your fill there. We have to stop at the tea shop downtown."

"And the shop with the olive oils and vinegars." Allie pulled a four-color brochure from her purse. She unfolded it to reveal a map of downtown Stillwater. "This is the path we usually take, Katie," she said, pointing in a way that looked as if she were building a Christmas tree from the bottom branches up.

"But one of the traditions we're busting this year is well-worn paths. So, today will look more like this," Bella said, reaching over the seat to draw an imaginary labyrinth on the map.

"The inefficiency of that plan," Elisa said, "makes my teeth hurt. But it'll be fun."

The Binder family seemed bulging with tradition. Didn't that come with an automatic resistance to change? If they hadn't booted Katie out yet, they probably wouldn't for her asking. "Busting traditions?"

"A family with no treasured traditions isn't very interesting," Allie said, refolding the brochure.

"But a family who holds traditions too tightly," Deb said, "sets itself up for disappointment. Sometimes the detours turn out better than the original plan."

"So, for as long as I can remember, we pick a couple of Binder Christmas traditions and turn them upside down each year." Elisa brushed something from Katie's shoulder as she talked. "Feather," she explained. "Down. Your coat's leaking."

Katie watched Rhonda leave the store, then stop to talk to someone on the street in front of the store and point as if giving directions.

"I heard Grandpa Wilson singing last night," Katie said.

"Yeah, that's one thing we miss out on because we're sleeping in the barn addition." Bella sighed.

Allie joined her. "That sweet man sings a verse of 'Amazing Grace' to Grandma Dodie every night before they fall asleep. Random verses. Not in any order. So precious. When we're here, he usually stands in the hall and sings it to all of us."

Rhonda settled into the driver's seat again. "Everybody still buckled up?"

Katie heard two clicks from the backseat.

Deb moaned loud enough for the whole van to hear. "The dumplings. One of us is going to have to learn how Grandma Dodie does it, so when she's gone . . ."

Wasn't Grandpa Wilson the one with the heart condition? Did they both have a serious medical issue? Maybe Deb projected long into the future. Katie caught herself caring more than she should, considering the soon-to-come conversation that would sever her ties with the whole family, not just Micah.

Something deep within her wanted to believe it could still work out, despite the evidence. The deep place groaned. She should have broken it off months ago to spare them both from the—

While the women chatted and the van made its way to their untraditional starting point, Katie wrestled with the truth she wanted to deny. If Katie got her heart's desire for Christmas—Micah and his family—then he couldn't have his—a long, stable marriage.

Rhonda parked the van in a municipal lot facing the river, with a clear view of the famed vertical lift bridge stretching across the St. Croix to Houlton, Wisconsin. She didn't turn off the engine, but sat, as did the rest of them, staring at the imposing structure.

"We have a vertical lift bridge on Highway 80 in Fort Myers," Katie said, determined to engage in normal Girls' Day conversation. "It's nothing like the size of this one."

"Kind of Stillwater's pride and embarrassment at the same time," Deb said. "How many years did it win 'Most Dangerous Bridge' honors?"

"You saw the new bridge they're perpetually working on about a mile south on your way through town, didn't you?" Allie waited for Katie's nod. "The locals are both grateful and heartbroken. Since what—the thirties?—the lift bridge has been a prime connecting point between this part of Minnesota and Wisconsin. In essence the lift bridge has been condemned since 2008. So, good news/bad news. New bridge. And because this vertical lift is on the National Register of Historic Places, it will serve out the remainder of its days as a walking and biking bridge."

Rhonda piped up. "We'd all be a lot healthier if we walked and biked more. I read an article this week about the effects of sitting on our—"

"Hold it!" Allie said. She stretched her arms spread-eagle.

The van stilled, except for the Christmas music still playing.

"Time out for this song," Allie said. No one objected.

Rhonda cranked the volume. Katie let the song's achingly beautiful music and lyrics stir her as the song always did. Hold me together. Forever near me. Pour over me . . . Mary's song of longing while carrying the Christ-child. By the time the song ended, tears flowed. Katie opened her eyes. She wasn't alone.

Deb opened her purse to distribute tissues to all in need.

The independence Katie's parents' decisions had forced on her served her well most of the time. But it also got in the way when she fought so hard to handle stress or distress on her own. In the past almost twenty-four hours, had she even once cried out "Hold me together!" to the only One who could?

The final notes of the song faded. Rhonda glanced back over her shoulder at her passengers. "Can I turn off the engine now?"

"No!" The entire backseat gave their opinion in unison. It would be three or more minutes before they exited the van, it looked like. The new song—a modern interpretation of what had become a classic in recent years—questioned whether the mother of Jesus realized the full implications of the Babe she carried.

The windows fogged over as six women allowed themselves to feel the eternal weight of the holiday many other people saw as a retailer's dream or an excuse to overindulge. At this rate, they might never get through their proposed labyrinth route for the day. They soaked in the moment as if settling into the meaning of the celebration rather than its ruckus. If Katie stayed another day, maybe more of it would rub off on her.

Which would net her more guilt—postponing the final breakup when she knew it could never work? Or disturbing their perfect Binder holiday and dragging Micah away from scenes like this because she had an ages-old problem?

She'd stay. Maybe not through the whole week, but at least until after Christmas Day.

Katie's treasures from the tea-and-spice shop weighed practically nothing. The vinegars and oils she'd purchased, however, might take careful packaging and rearranging to keep her luggage from overshooting the fifty-pound limit. She'd probably regret the expenditures, in light of what she owed.

The peach balsamic begged for a chance to dress a salad or marinate pork chops, Micah's favorite. The basil oil screamed pasta. Her apartment's toy-sized kitchen and hat-sized grill would get a workout when she got home.

"I wonder if we'll have time to come back through town at night," Allie said as they dodged foot traffic on the sidewalks on their way to another destination. "Rock Point Church has a Christmas light show during the winter. The street leading up to the church is lined with lighted trees that turn on and off to Christmas music."

"Where's Rhonda?" Deb turned to look behind them. "Tying her boot laces. Slow down, everybody."

"We could split up and then meet somewhere later," Katie suggested.

"Tried that once," Allie said. "Made us miserable not to see the expressions on each others' faces when we saw something intriguing or found a piece of art that one of us from the other group would have enjoyed."

Rhonda caught up. The women resumed their pace.

Bella turned and walked backward while she said, "You have to come in summer sometime, Katie."

Allie tugged Bella out of the way of oncoming foot traffic. Bella dropped back beside Katie.

"The Binder Summer Reunion is amazing too. Tougher for everyone to get off work, but so much fun," Bella said.

Katie considered the concept of a summer version of the crammed cottage with swimming replacing ice skating and cookouts taking the place of chicken and dumplings.

"Summer in Stillwater. The trolley tours start up again," Bella said. "The thirteen-passenger bike—a riot."

"And Micah could take you on a Venetian gondola ride on the river," Elisa said. "That would be romantic."

"The surrey rides are romantic too," Bella added.

"Or," Rhonda said, "the walking path along the river. You can easily log ten thousand steps a day walking along the river. Or the Stillwater Steps. Now, that's a workout." She hopped on one foot and hiked up her pant leg. "See these calf muscles? Stillwater Steps."

"Aunt Rhonda, she's not looking for a workout. She's looking for romance." She was? Micah already had a gift for creating romantic moments.

"Mom, do you think we'll have time for the Victorian Christmas at the courthouse today?" Elisa slapped her mittened hands together to match the pleading on her face.

"We'll see. Grandma Dodie's stamina just isn't what it once was."

"Katie, you would love, love, love that. It's an 1870 Italianate courthouse. Micah would know all the details better than the tour guide, I bet."

So his cousins were in awe of his penchant for historical trivia too? Katie wasn't the only one who saw that in him? "What are you two studying?" she asked, charmed by their lack of pretense and the twin-like synchronization that replaced what could easily have been sibling rivalry.

"Elisa's English Lit," Bella said. "I'm 'Undeclared.'"

"I remember those days," Katie said. "So many options."

"The best thing about college so far?" Bella said. "My suite-mates, and this. Christmas break."

As they exited another must-see shop, Deb and Katie wound up side-by-side at the rear of the pack. Conversation flowed so freely from Allie's daughters. Deb's waters ran deep and rarely bubbled to the surface. After a few too-quiet moments, Katie said, "Micah's dad's surgery did turn out okay, didn't it?"

Deb hesitated. She adjusted her purse to her other shoulder. "Yes. He has to go back every six months for retesting. That's coming up in February. We take one day at a time."

Katie nodded, but knew she was in the company of people far more expert at that skill than she was.

"I'll trade you stories," Deb said.

"What do you mean?"

"You mentioned being an only child since kindergarten. I didn't realize you'd had a sibling at one time."

"A sister. She was two years older than me."

"Oh, Katie."

"The best medical care. She died anyway. And there I was. The inadequate one."

Deb put her arm around her. "You can't think that way."

The moment passed without comment. Deb was right. Katie had been trying to convince herself of the same thing since she was five years old.

Allie called back, "Let's aim for LoLo's and get something to eat. The heavy lunch crowd should have thinned by now."

"Mom, nobody 'thins' at LoLo's. And the crowd doesn't either."

"Good point, Bella," Rhonda said. "But they do have vegan and gluten-free options and because it's Christmas Week, I'm having smoked French fries."

The logic escaped Katie, but she followed the others toward the restaurant where she and Micah had killed time the day before.

The women discussed menu options at LoLo's while waiting for Rhonda to extricate Grandma Dodie from Darn. Knit. Anyway. Even menu choices stirred laughter among these people Katie might have chosen for friends if they'd met under other circumstances.

She sipped water poured from a glass-stoppered bottle while she studied the appetizer and entrée descriptions. Her decision made, she looked out at a crowd different from yet similar to the one she and Micah had seen through the same window the day before. A sudden rustle of commotion caught her attention. She bolted from her chair and grabbed her coat.

"Someone fell," Katie called back, heading for the entrance. It didn't look like Grandma Dodie, but she couldn't be sure until she got closer.

The crowd around the fallen one parted when Katie mentioned her profession. An older woman—maybe seventy—sat on the sidewalk with her back against the lamppost.

"I stepped off the curb funny, Walter. That's all. Now help me up. Please."

"Hi. I'm Katie Vale. I'm a nurse practitioner. Can you tell me what happened? And what hurts? And your name?" Could have handled that more smoothly.

"Patricia Whitfield," Walter said.

"I know my own name." Patricia pushed with her hands to lift herself from the sitting position, unsuccessfully. "The young woman wants to check on my faculties, Walter. Let me do the talking."

"Yes, dear."

"Anna Whitfield. And all I did was slip on the curb. My knee must have given out again. I'm fine."

Anna? Her husband said Patricia. Katie automatically performed her traditional visual assessment. Color, respiration rate, use of extremities, pupils. Hmm. She checked for a medical information bracelet. None. "Did you have any sense of dizziness before you fell?"

"Yes, she did."

"I can answer for myself, Walter." The look in her eyes told Katie so much. "Just a touch."

"She's had this sort of thing happen before."

"Walter."

"Hush." The frail man filled his lungs and said, "I'll tell the lady what she really needs to hear. Yes, she must have been dizzy. She staggered a little before she slipped."

"My head's fine," Patricia said. "It's my ankle."

Knee? Ankle? Katie looked from her crouching position to the bystanders. She caught Deb's attention and mouthed, "Call 9-1-1."

Deb nodded and pulled one of the crowd members away from the scene toward the window. Ah. The no-technology week for the Binders. Deb had to borrow someone else's phone.

"May I remove your boot, Anna?" Katie asked. "I'll be gentle." She chose to use the name the woman used. No need to send her into defense mode.

"Anna? No. That's the character I play in the church pageant. My name's Patricia."

Katie slid the woman's foot out of a boot that wouldn't be loose much longer. Her ankle had already started to swell. Katie snatched her borrowed knit hat out of her coat pocket and asked Walter to fill it with snow from the small piles left over from the sidewalk shovelers. Katie tucked it around the swollen ankle.

"Can you squeeze my hand, Patricia?" Katie asked, holding the improvised ice pack with her right hand and extending her left.

"Of course I can." She squeezed.

"How about this one?" Katie picked up Patricia's left hand. Marked difference. More than could be explained by hand dominance.

"Just let me get up off this cold ground. I'm fine." The woman's voice trembled as Walter's had. "Besides, I have company coming in a few hours. No time for this nonsense."

Katie put her palm on Patricia's cool, soft cheek. Cool. Good. "Patricia, don't you want to be able to enjoy your company without worrying that something more might be going on? We know for sure your ankle needs more attention. And you can't afford another dizzy spell while you're taking the ham out of the oven, now can you?"

"We're having crown roast." The woman's pout softened a degree.

"Do you make corn bread stuffing or do you use stale bread?"

"I know what you're doing. You're keeping me talking so I don't notice that siren in the distance. And it's coming for me, isn't it?"

Katie adjusted the makeshift ice pack so it put little pressure on the ankle itself. "It's the wise thing to do, Patricia. Just let the professionals check it all out and send you into your holiday plans with your mind at ease. And Walter's."

The woman's face scrunched. "I have . . . so much . . . to get done."

"Nothing that won't wait for you. It might be the year to turn some traditions upside down."

Patricia's expression grew stern. "Whoever heard of such a thing?"

Katie smiled up at Walter, who held his wife's right boot and enormous cobalt blue purse. The siren drew nearer.

"Any allergies, Patricia?"

"Yes. I'm allergic to changes in my plans." Her sly grin seemed more pronounced on one side than the other.

Katie asked the crowd to make way for the paramedics as the boxy ambulance pulled to a stop a few feet from the action. One of the busiest intersections in Stillwater grew busier as the team took over.

They debriefed Katie about what she'd observed. Another local, one of Walter's friends, offered to take him to the medical center where the ambulance headed with Patricia safely tucked inside. The crowd resumed its normal Christmas bustle and ambiance. Deb gave Katie a hug and walked her back inside the restaurant.

"Are you all finished?" Katie asked, noting the blank place settings in front of each Binder.

"We waited for you," Grandma Dodie said. "Praying, mostly. Our poor waiter is going to need a significant tip. He's been to our table six times refilling our drinks."

"I'm so sorry to hold you up. I assumed you'd go ahead and order." She and Deb took the last two chairs at the table.

"Katie, your hands are like icicles," Deb said. "Here." She slid a cup of hot tea toward Katie. "Don't know whose it is, but it'll do for a hand warmer."

"Thanks. You never know when a little adventure will

strike." Katie closed her hands around the cup and shrugged her neck deeper into her sweater.

"Jeremy," Grandma Dodie called out. "Soup! Bring us soup!"

"I guess we're all having soup," Elisa said, chuckling, and turning her menu upside down.

"For starters," Grandma Dodie said. "It appears"—she clasped her hands to her heart and directed her words to Katie—"we're all going to need our strength these days."

Deb gave Katie another quick hug. "Proud of you, Katie. You handled that so well."

"It's my job," she said. "Not that exact scene." She indicated the street now filling with as many people as fresh snowflakes. "I must say, I've never had a cold pack source that close before. Whose hat did I borrow? It's on the way to the clinic right now."

"Take my tea. Take my hat. Take my cousin . . ." Bella said, a hint of her father's voice in her words.

"You're sure it's okay for me to take Jericho out this afternoon, Grandpa Wilson?"

That Micah. Hard to say no to that boy. How had Katie done it? Looked him right in the eye and told him she wasn't going to marry him. Strong woman behind all that delicate. "Told you, Micah, it's fine with me. Good to get him some fresh air and sunshine. Good for all of us. The neighbor boy helps with that when he's around. Kids' schedules fill up fast these days."

"True for all of us. No matter our age. Life gets too busy with things that aren't all that important," Micah said, a crease forming in his forehead.

"You doing okay down there in alligator country?"

He chuckled. "We don't see many alligators near Fort Myers, Grandpa. Yeah, I'm doing . . . okay."

"Have you given any more thought to what I told you? Your grandma and I will find a way to help out, if you want to start on grad school. Whatever it takes, Micah."

"It's not a good time right now."

Should I say it right out? Or keep my nose out of the boy's business? "Micah, sometimes those who are the most generous have an issue letting others be generous with them. And, I mean, a heart issue." There. He'd said it. He watched Micah's expression for evidence that he'd pushed too hard.

"It's more blessed to give than to receive, right, Grandpa Wilson?"

He would need two deep breaths for this one. "But if we aren't willing to receive, aren't we keeping someone else from a blessing then? Seems kind of selfish, doesn't it? And I know that's not who you've ever been."

Micah scrunched his mouth, obviously chagrined. Score one for the old man.

CHAPTER SIX

DEB SUGGESTED SHE AND KATIE walk from the restaurant to their next stop, one of many antique shop options in downtown Stillwater. The rest waited for Rhonda to pick them up in the van. Katie's suspicions that Micah's mom had prearranged their alone time as an opportunity to have a talk with her were quickly confirmed.

"Kind of tough to be thrown into a family like this at Christmastime, isn't it." Deb looped her infinity scarf around her neck as they walked.

"To be fair, I didn't make it any easier on everybody. But they've been"—Katie searched for the word she wanted—"storybook wonderful."

Deb laughed. "You won't believe me when I tell you this, but that's the exact word I used to describe the Binders when I first started dating Tim. I didn't grow up in a family like this."

"You already know I didn't either," Katie said. "Not even close."

"It took me a long time to realize Tim's family members were genuine. About everything. Their love for one another.

Their 'live each moment to the full because it might be the last' philosophy. Their faith."

"I'm more reserved than most of the Binders." *Reserved. Let's call it that.*

"I'm still reserved, as you may have noticed, Katie." Deb smiled her direction. "But I eventually let go of the resistance that was standing between us."

Is that what she thought Katie's problem was? Resistance?

"I'd be the last person to pressure you, Katie. I know what it's like to find all the hugs and intense love for one another a little overwhelming."

Deb knew. She knew. Something inside Katie's chest relaxed.

"But I'd also hate for you to miss out on what it's like to be embraced more fully than you could have imagined. Championed. Included. Loved no matter what."

"Is that what you found?"

Deb's chin disappeared into her scarf for a moment. "The first time Tim's folks invited me to dinner, Dodie hugged me and told me she loved me. The first time. I hadn't heard those words from my own parents since—" She slowed her pace. "I still haven't. Not unsolicited. They'll say it if I speak the words first. Sometimes."

Deb picked up the pace again. Even with the press of people on the street, Katie heard her muffled sigh. "It's not the same."

Deb could smile as broadly as any of the natural-born

Binders. She loved as strongly. Laughed in sync with them. Acted the epitome of kindness. But her childhood didn't train her for this. How did she make the transition? And what did she put Tim through in the early days of their relationship? Was he right now counseling Micah how to survive a woman like Katie?

A guy shouldn't have to go through survival training to love someone.

Katie had the power to spare him that. Should. Right after Christmas. Katie had enough memories of holidays turned sour with heartbreak. And she had enough respect for the meaning of holy days to exert what little willpower she had to postpone the inevitable a few more days.

"Katie? Did you hear that?"

She reined her thoughts back to Main Street, Stillwater. Still. Water. Still waters. Two days from Christmas and she wasn't thinking of Luke's verses about shepherds abiding in the fields but a psalm of a Shepherd leading her to still waters. "Hear what?"

Deb pointed toward the waterfront now visible as they crossed the intersection. On the street that hugged the river, a slow-moving pair of beefy horses pulled a ruby-red mini-wagon driven by a man whose snowy beard looked completely legit. Naturally padded belly too.

Katie stopped when they topped the far curb so she could watch the horse-drawn wagon's progress. Happy families and young couples and others closer to Grandma and Grandpa

Binder's age waved from the small wagon. "That looks like fun." *Focus on the fun, Katie.*

Deb kept moving. "Can I tell you a secret?"

Katie pulled her eyes from the charming scene to catch up with her guide. Buildings soon blocked the view that had captured her. "Sure."

"Don't let the Chamber of Commerce hear me say this, but I prefer Stillwater in the off seasons. When it's quieter. Fewer people. There's still plenty of activity to choose from. And the beauty of this place never dies."

The group reunited at the Staples Mill shops after their brief separation. The next hour ticked by with a trip down history's aisles. Christmas-themed antiques took center stage just inside the doors and in the window displays of several of the shops the group of women visited. Although drawn to a vintage nativity set and antique bubble lights, Katie bypassed the holiday memories and walked deeper into each store. She started at the back and worked her way forward. She moved in and out of range of the others. When she drew close, she observed the Binder women's ease with one another and delight over their "finds," most of which they enjoyed, discussed, then walked past, as if owning were not as important as celebrating the item's existence.

Katie shared that in common with them. For a brief moment, the thought made her feel like part of the family. How could a single thought both warm and terrify her?

A display of antique brooches caught her eye.

"When I get married," Elisa said, leaning over Katie's shoulder, "I'm going to make my bridal bouquet out of antique pins and brooches. I saw a couple of brooch bouquets on Pinterest. Gorgeous. Plus it would last forever."

Forever.

"You can keep shopping if you want," Grandma Dodie said, leaning on a distressed Hoosier cabinet. "But I think it's time for me to get off this leg. Rhonda, would you mind taking me home?"

The women all agreed they'd seen enough and were ready to head back to the cottage together. They took a short detour to a corner grocery store for two gallons of milk, then wound their way north to Lubber's Lane.

"The men are cooking tonight," Grandma Dodie said from the front passenger seat. "Should be interesting."

"Micah's a great cook," Katie said. "As long as the heat source is an outdoor grill."

"Or campfire," Deb added. "Speaking of which—"

"The boys are already on the case," Dodie assured them.

Katie waited for someone to explain. Allie leaned over the seat and offered, "Bonfire tonight. One of my favorite events during Christmas Week."

"Bonfire?"

"Down by the pond every year," Elisa said. "Unless it's a year without snow."

"So," Katie ventured, "you roast marshmallows and sing a Christmas version of 'Kum-baya'?" Katie tried to imagine which Christmas carol most closely mimicked "Kum-baya" and decided it might not have been written yet.

Deb turned toward Katie as much as her seat belt would allow. "Different kind of bonfire. We burn the past year's regrets."

Rhonda pulled the van close to the back door of the cottage to give Grandma Dodie the best chance of getting into the house without slipping and falling. "If I'd worn my Sorrel boots," she said, "instead of these flimsy things, you could have parked behind the barn and I would have walked."

"Mmm, not today, Mom." The look on Deb's face stirred Katie's diagnostic instincts. Had Deb seen something in Grandma Dodie's coloring or gait or breathing that Katie had missed? Entirely possible, as consumed as Katie had been with her own problems. Self-focused. She'd learned it at home from practiced professionals. And there it was again. Self-absorption. She turned her attention to clearing the way from the van to the back door, kicking a chunk of a fallen icicle from the path and making sure the mudroom entry was free of boots and other winter gear.

"Ohhh," Grandma Dodie said as she stepped into the cottage. Her word lingered, not like a cry of pain, but as if she'd just gotten an inside joke or hidden message. "Yes. Yes, leave the van right there for now. Katie, let me take your purchases and put them someplace safe. I have a small favor to ask you."

Take your blood pressure? Test the grip strength of your extremities?

"Would you take these shriveled carrots out to Jericho in the barn? They're no good to us, but he'll love them."

Jericho. The horse.

"I haven't been around horses much."

"Jericho is as gentle as they come. Go on. You might want something warmer on your head, though." She pulled a red knit hat from the tote bag where she kept her knitting.

"It has my name on it!" Katie fingered the white stitching that matched the hats of all the real Binder grandchildren.

"Good thing you women didn't get me for lunch a minute sooner or your name would have been missing the *e*."

Katie felt the soft, thick yarn and thicker-still ribbing, the stitches uneven enough to mark it as hand-knit. "Thank you."

"I know you won't have much call for it in Florida, but when you come back here, it'll be waiting for you."

Oh, Grandma Dodie. Katie hoped the threads of the embroidered name could be snipped off and the hat reused for someone else.

The other women skirted past Grandma Dodie and Katie, on their way to other projects. Katie pulled on the hat, which covered her ears and forehead well, and took the limp carrots Grandma Dodie offered.

"Go around by the back entrance to the barn. Then you won't spook him."

Katie didn't relish the idea of a horse that spooked easily.

“There are a few deer apples in a bucket by the barn entrance, too, Katie. He loves those,” Deb called from the doorway between the kitchen and family room.

Apparently, she had one more family member to meet. A horse.

She crossed the space between the cottage and the barn. The snow glistened as if a quadrillion LED lights lay buried under its surface. Such pure colors—the white snow, stark red barn, crayon-blue sky. She rounded the corner of the barn and came nose to nose with the nicker she’d heard.

The horse shook his head, rattling his bridle and the jingling bells attached to a leather strap. Who wouldn’t jump back with an animal that size shaking its head at the sight of her?

“Katie, Jericho is harmless. More overgrown kitten than horse.” Micah’s voice soothed, as it always did.

She ducked around the massive beast’s head and found Micah standing beside a pull-down step on a black two-person sleigh with a deep red, deeply tufted interior.

“Your carriage awaits,” he said.

The chestnut horse’s flank shivered. “He’s wearing a diaper?”

“We call it a diaper bag. Or a bun bag. So as not to hurt his feelings.” Micah winked. “Believe me, you’ll be grateful for it. Climb in. Nice hat.”

“Thanks.” After some searching, she found good handholds on the sleigh and stepped in, with Micah’s help. The lush velvet interior showed signs of wear, as did the black paint. How long had it been in the family? "Oh wait. I have these," she said, dangling the shriveled carrots in front of Micah's nose as he climbed in beside her.

"Nice. If you prefer that to the snacks I packed to bring along—"

"Very funny. They're for Jericho."

At the mention of his name, the animal turned his head, one large, dark eye glaring at her.

"You made him very happy."

Katie tucked the sleigh's lap robe around her legs, carrots still in hand. "That's happy?"

"No. This is." Micah wrapped one arm around her, cupped her chin, and tilted his head to the side to kiss her. Tenderly, as he always did.

When the kiss ended, Katie stifled the urge to grab fistfuls of his coat and pull him back toward her. Her heart pounded in her throat. It beat a rhythm that said, *Please, Micah. Don't let go.* The pounding in her brain overrode that self-absorbed noise.

"Got it!"

The two in the sleigh turned toward the speaker. Uncle Paul. With a camera. Standing just a few feet behind them. "You'll love that shot. It will make a great engagement picture. Or maybe next year's photo Christmas card. Have fun, you two." Paul worked his way around the sleigh on Katie's side. "Are these yours?" he asked her, retrieving carrots from the snow. She didn't remember dropping them. It must have been the kiss.

He gave Jericho's shoulder a pat. "See you in an hour or so? We're cooking tonight, Micah."

"I remember. Does the pizza place deliver this far out?"

"Not sure Grandma Dodie would go for that. Homemade pizzas, maybe. Christmas-themed." Uncle Paul fed the carrots to the horse then left them alone, stopping to snap two more pictures.

Micah picked up the reins and said, "Don't worry, Katie. We have a plan."

So do I. And neither one of us is going to like it, judging from that kiss.

The sleigh runners made a shooshing sound as they slid along the snow on Lubber's Lane. Jericho's slow, plow-horse pace kept the sound low-pitched. The afternoon sun fought hard to warm the scene between the fingers of trees in its way. The blanket helped. Micah's arm around her helped more.

"Can you talk and drive at the same time, Micah?"

He lifted the reins to show that Jericho needed little nudging from him. It was as if the horse knew the route. "It's not like texting and driving. Yes, I can talk. What's on your mind?"

So much. Too much. "What do you really want out of life?"

"We're starting with the easy questions, huh?"

"I'm serious."

Jericho eased them down an incline then dug into the snow-packed back road to climb the next hill.

"What do I want out of life?" He took the reins with both hands. "A faster horse?"

"Wrong answer."

"Jericho's not very fast, you may have noticed."

"Cut him some slack, Micah," Katie teased. "He's doing the best he can for an animal his age. How old is he?"

"Older than I am."

Katie shifted to face him. "How long do horses live?"

"About this long. But back to your original question . . ."

Easygoing, but without the irresponsibility that accompanies too many easygoing people. One more thing to love about Micah. To love. To lose?

"What do I really want out of life? Besides you?" he asked.

She studied the stitching on the leather gloves she wore. A lose thread. She tugged on it to tighten the gap, but two more stitches worked lose. Better to cut it off. "Besides me."

"A great family Christmas . . . with you. A new year full of adventure . . . with you. A lifetime . . . with you. Babies . . . with you."

"Micah!"

"Eventually."

He wasn't making this easier. "Micah, if you could have any job or pursuit in the world, what would you want to be doing?"

"You've asked this before."

"And you've never given me an answer that didn't sound like a comedy routine."

He flicked the reins. Jericho responded by keeping his one-note pace, lifting his tail and dropping something into the diaper bag.

"There's another word for that," Micah said. "Although . . ."

"Would you be serious for a minute? Please?"

At the crest of a hill, with a panoramic view of the St. Croix River unobstructed by trees in this one spot, Micah pulled back on the reins. That command, Jericho obeyed. The soft clop of horse hooves stopped, as did the constant shooshing sound of the sleigh runners.

Micah said nothing. He stared ahead, then down.

"I read a lot," Katie said, her voice barely registering in the winter quiet.

"I know. I love that about you."

"It frustrates me when I read a novel about a conflict between people that goes on and on when all they'd need to do is sit down and talk to each other for a few minutes. And listen to each other."

He faced her then. "Don't I always listen to you? Most of the time?"

"You're a good listener."

"Then . . ."

"We have things to talk about that neither one of us has been willing to address."

"What things?" His man-face turned to boy-face. He

closed his eyes a moment, then reinstalled his man-face. "What things, Katie?"

"Tell me what you want to do with your life. It matters for the discussion."

Jericho stomped one hoof and rattled his harness, then settled into an almost catatonic state.

"If I had no limitations . . . ?"

"No limitations." She drew the lap robe under her chin for warmth.

"I would go back to college, get my master's, and teach history in a charter school or private school."

She expelled a quick breath. "Huh. You finally said it out loud."

"I've hinted."

The cords on the sides of Katie's throat tightened. "Why didn't you do that in the first place? Go back to college."

Micah toyed with the tips of the leather reins. "Thought about it. Then circumstances got in the way. And then I met you."

I'm not—no woman is—a good enough reason not to fulfill your dreams, Micah. "What circumstances?"

"The truth?"

"The truth. And nothing but the truth."

Micah's exhale left a cloud of discomfort in the crisp air. "Adoption is expensive."

Where did that come from?

"My sister and her husband will make great parents. I wish you could have met them."

A bald eagle braved the cold air and soared across Katie's field of vision. What did the expense of adoption have to do with—? "You paid for their adoption costs? Micah!"

"Not all of them. That would have been, like, forty-five thousand dollars. The rest of the family pooled together to kick in the other half."

"You bought them a baby." The thought pressed her against the back of the tufted velvet.

"God gave them a baby. I helped with expenses. This has been such a long haul for them. International adoptions are tricky and expensive. But Courtney and Brogan really wanted to adopt from Korea in honor of Grandpa Wilson. He served there with the Marines. Grandma Dodie has pictures of him with Korean orphans when his company handed out candy at Christmas. It's always been on Courtney's heart. But, as I said, quite an expense."

"And that was your history teacher college fund."

"Basically. Plus a little more. I started saving again. And then the ring. So I'm back up to almost seventy-five dollars toward my goal." He laughed as if it were a laughing matter. The Binder take-life-as-it-comes and cherish-every-moment-good-or-bad laughter.

He'd given away everything he had that would have helped get him what he really wanted out of life. So much for waiting until after Christmas. It had to happen now. "Micah, that's all the more reason I can't"—no determination would keep the tears from falling—"marry you. I can't."

"Did you see them take off, Tim?" Wilson dipped his teabag in the hot water. None of that fancy loose-leaf stuff the women liked. Plain old black all-American tea. Or, maybe not all-American, but strong enough to be mistaken for coffee. Although the caffeine played tricks on his brain lately. Not jittery, exactly . . .

"No," Tim said. "But Paul took pictures as they got ready to leave. That sleigh needs some work, Dad."

"Some things are better a little rough around the edges."

Tim smiled. "You're right. Who would argue with that idea?" He tugged at small tufts of his hair. "I'll be as white-haired as you are before long."

"Two gray hairs do not count as rough and weathered, my boy."

"I love you."

Wilson lowered his gaze. "One can't hear that too much. Especially . . ."

"Dad. Ancient history."

Ancient history that wormed its way into present life all too often. "Noted. I appreciate the reminder. And your grace."

"Learned it from you and Mom."

"Mostly from your mom."

Tim took Wilson's cup of tea. "Let me carry this into the family room for you."

"Guess I filled it a little full, didn't I?" *God bless you, boy, for not blaming the shakiness.*

Tonight, he'd sing:

Through many dangers, toils and snares,

I have already come;

'Tis grace hath brought me safe thus far,

And grace will lead me home.

Dodie would like that. She always said that verse was one of her favorites. And he knew why.

CHAPTER SEVEN

WAS A COLD FRONT EXPECTED? The air chilled while Katie waited for a response to her insistence that marriage was an impossibility for them. For her.

"You mean right now, don't you?" Micah said. "You can't marry me right now, when I'm broke. That's it."

"Do you really think I'm that shallow? That's not it at all."

"Then what?" Micah looped the reins around a handhold in front of him and stuffed his hands under his armpits.

"Because I'm the opposite of what you need. I would stand in the way of everything important to you."

"You're important to me." He reached for her hands under the lap robe. "Katie, you have to know that by now."

"It's what you don't know about me that creates the problem."

"Serial killer?"

"No!" She slapped at his sleeve.

"Allergic to my aftershave?"

"You shave?" She couldn't help herself. His humor sometimes irritated but usually defused her angst.

"Then what? And I quote, 'Most conflicts could be resolved if people would just sit down and talk to each other. And listen. And kiss once in a while.'"

"Not a direct quote."

"Close enough."

Katie, it's now or never. "You want longevity in marriage. I can't promise you that."

"I don't want longevity. I want forever."

"There you go. My family doesn't do forever."

Micah put his arm around her. "I know your parents had a miserable marriage, but—"

"It's not just my parents. I can trace back almost two hundred years on my mother's side and not find a married couple that stayed together. They divorced, or one left the other one, or shot the other one, or they stayed single, or they married but had no children . . ."

"Any upstanding citizens at all?"

"Oh, sure," Katie said. "A mayor, a doctor, a woman who single-handedly established a library system for rural communities shortly after the Civil War, teachers and lawyers and nurses and construction workers. But relationally? A mess. How can one family line have so many people who couldn't figure out how to make marriage work?"

"What does that have to do with you and me?"

"Micah, honestly. Your family has this thing perfected. The Binders have probably never uttered the words *divorce* or *separation* or *custody hearings* or *abandonment.* Your lineage probably traces back through centuries of syrupy sweet bliss. And besides . . ."

"Go on." The tinge of irritation in his voice was new.

This part would be at least as hard to admit. "One of the 'gifts' my parents gave me was letting me know—about a month after I passed my boards—that they were bequeathing me my school loan debt. They said the divorce cost too much. It was ten years before I graduated, but whatever. So they agreed on something one time, once—to cut me off and leave me to pay the whole thing."

"I'm so sorry. It will take a while to pay off, but an education is—"

"Micah, during college, I used my summers to volunteer. I went on mission trips and worked at the free clinic when I wasn't in classes instead of getting paying jobs because I believed what my parents promised. And I know. I know how many parents can't afford to help their kids with college costs. I completely understand that."

Micah rubbed her arm. She barely felt it through the layers of sweater and coat and resistance.

"The fault lies in me because I depended on them, trusted in a promise from people I already knew had a hard time keeping promises. Maybe it was immaturity on my part. Maybe wishful thinking. Maybe I wanted so badly to believe that their investment in me for my schooling equaled a depth of emotional investment I'd craved too long." She pinched back tears. "Young children aren't the only ones affected by divorce."

"Makes sense. I can't imagine not having parents I could trust to be on my side."

"That's not the end of my financial tale of woe." She pressed the back of a limp hand against her forehead to underscore "tale of woe" and glanced at him to gauge his response. "I bought a house soon after I first landed my job—before I knew about inheriting my school debt, and then had to sell it at the most awful time in the real estate economy, which meant taking a huge loss on the sale. And yes, I know that makes me an idiot."

Micah slid his arm from where it had rested behind her and held his head in his hands, elbows on his knees.

"See? I'm the opposite of what you need. Bad ancestry. Bad decisions. Bad credit. Bad debt . . ."

"I'll take it."

"What?"

"All of it." He raised his head, his eyes brimming. "I'm looking forward to spending my life with someone who came from that and turned out like this. Warm. Loving. Caring. Strong. Capable. Smart."

She turned toward him. "Micah, I have $80,000 worth of debt and have barely made a dent in it!"

"We'll conquer it together."

"I knew you'd say that. It's the kind of man you are. But doing so would keep you from your dream."

"From the career part of my dream. Not the heart's desire part."

Katie threw the lap robe on the floor of the sleigh. "I can't do that to you. And I can't let you do that to yourself."

"Are you done talking?"

"For now."

"Good. Because something's not right with Jericho. Is it just me, or is he listing to the right?"

"I didn't know horses could make snow angels." Twilight pressed her nose against the glass as she knelt on Katie's window seat in the kitchen.

Grandma Binder called the child to the stove. "I need your help listening for the timer for the brownies, Twilight."

"But—"

"Grandma said."

"Yes, ma'am."

Grandma Dodie gave her granddaughter an extra-tight hug. "Your daddy and uncles are making supper for us, but we all know who makes the best brownies, don't we?"

"You and me."

"You and I. That's right." She squeezed again.

Katie turned her attention to the smeared mixing bowl in the sink and the hot, soapy water soaking away the mess as she swirled the dishcloth. Cleaning the baking tools was the least she could do after killing off their horse.

It may not have been her fault, directly. But if she hadn't insisted Micah stop the sleigh, they might have made it all the way back to the barn before Jericho collapsed. As it was, he lay stiff-legged on his side in the snow between the barn and the cottage, in full view of little eyes who'd now seen a horse make an unnaturally stiff snow angel.

"Is Jericho dead, Grandma?"

Katie held her breath for the answer.

"Jericho finished his life, sweetie. And what a good life he had."

The answer must have landed softly on Twilight's ears. They raked Katie's soul . . . both for the much-loved animal and for the aged humans nearing life's end.

"Will we have a funeral?"

Katie stopped making noise with the dishwater.

"It's a pretty busy week, little one. Tomorrow is Christmas Eve."

Katie didn't turn to see if Twilight had her hands on her hips, but her voice sounded like it. "Grandma, I don't think Jesus would mind. He's good at sharing."

"You're right. He is. The best. I'll tell you what. I'll talk to your mom and dad and your aunts and uncles and see if we can have a memorial service for Jericho during our bonfire tonight."

"That would be perfect!" Twilight said. "I'm going to write a poem."

"Great idea."

"About dying at Christmas," the little girl said.

If Katie had been chewing gum, she would have swallowed it. Instead, she choked and coughed.

"Or . . ." Grandma Dodie offered, "a poem about horses making snow angels."

Katie spoke up. "That sounds like a beautiful idea."

"Aunt Katie, can you listen for the oven timer for Grandma? I want to go get started."

Another beautiful idea. "Yes. Go ahead. I'll take over for you." She didn't have the heart to correct the "aunt" part.

In a house that congested, it seemed curious that Grandma Dodie and Katie were left alone in the kitchen.

"I'm perfectly capable of listening for the timer myself, Katie, if you want to go do something else."

"Here is good. I'd rather not be outside when the horse funeral director arrives with his truck. I'm so sorry about Jericho." Katie sat at the table and raked her fingers through her hat hair.

"He was a good horse. Want some tea?"

"No thanks. Wait. Yes. I'd love some."

"A good horse, but too much for Wilson to take care of anymore." Grandma Dodie paused, lost in a thought Katie could only imagine. "I'm grateful we didn't have to make a decision about giving him away or having him put down. He lived longer than any horse has a right to expect."

Katie took the cup she offered. "It was the sleigh ride, wasn't it? We shouldn't have taken him out."

"If not that, it would have been something else." She lowered herself into the chair at the end of the table. "Don't take this on your own shoulders, dear."

"I feel so bad."

"Well," Dodie said, rising to respond to the oven timer, "you only have to hold on to that, if you insist, for another few hours."

The smell of newborn brownies filled the kitchen. "A few hours?"

"The bonfire. A little horse funeral and a little regret burning."

The men's supper preparations got a late start, considering the need to say their farewells to Jericho, whose walls had come tumbling down as soon as Micah released him from his harness.

Katie watched the Binders move in and out of soberness over the family's loss and buoyancy of gratitude for Jericho's life and tenderness of memories, without losing touch with the undercurrent of joy marked by strings of lights and the ever-present Christmas carols. There it came again—the carol Katie found hauntingly comforting. It had become her favorite of the looping playlist. "All Is Well."

Its message fought hard to convince her it spoke truth. That despite everything, she was loved. Despite everything, hope kept flickering like a trick birthday candle that refused to go out. Or the LED candles Grandma Dodie kept in every road-facing window, spilling a path of light across the snow, shining even brighter the darker the night became.

By the time the last of the dishes had been cleared—still

the men's assignment despite the new snow that had fallen in the night—Rhonda and Allie were already headed to the edge of the pond, where earlier in the day the men had stacked wood for the bonfire.

After their first meal together, cleanup had been decided in the traditional Binder way—by snowfall accumulation. Grandma Dodie measured the snow depth with her yardstick. If it was closer to an even number, the women did the dishes. If closer to an odd number, the men won the honor. So far, it was coming out odd whether it snowed or not.

The women had the fire blazing by the time the rest of the family hauled patio chairs and folding chairs for the older members and laid a ring of logs for the more agile. The night air felt like stepping into the walk-in freezer in the research lab at the hospital. The fire drew everyone closer to its comfort.

"You'll need this," Micah said, draping an old quilt over her shoulders.

"Does it come in an electric version?" Katie asked. The temps must have dropped dramatically in the last few hours.

"Imagine white sand beaches so sun-heated you can't walk on them barefoot."

Katie smiled as he settled into a chair beside her. "Still not feeling it."

"Aunt Katie, try this." Aurora spread her quilt wide and high behind her, as if capturing heat from the fire like a sail would capture wind. She held it that way for a few seconds, then tightened it around her like a cocoon.

"Or, try this," Micah said, scooting his chair closer and wrapping both arms around her.

"Yeah, that's better," Aurora said.

Katie expected the ten-year-old to affect an "Ewww!" No lack of surprises with the Binders. Including Micah's arms around her after their abbreviated but serious-as-they-come talk.

Twilight sat on Grandpa Wilson's lap, with one arm around his neck, as she read her "Why We'll Miss You, Jericho" poem. The grammar and rhyming could have used some editing, but the sentiment hit home.

Family members stared into the fire, wordless, after Twilight's tribute. Katie imagined the internal thoughts ranged from "That was sweet" to "What will we say when Grandpa Wilson's or Grandma Dodie's gone?" to "I wonder if there are any brownies left."

Katie's thoughts followed a different path. Micah needed time to think about what she'd said. Time to process what it meant. She needed to give him time. With all the activity swirling on the property, that wasn't likely to happen until the holiday was over. Maybe it would hit him full-force on their plane ride home. She wouldn't be able to hide out in the bathroom there.

"Make the most of every opportunity." Wasn't there a Bible verse that said that? She'd been given the rare opportunity to be enveloped in a loving family's Christmas celebrations. She'd let the hitch in her relationship with Micah—a hitch he seemed content to ignore for the moment—keep her from recognizing the gift she'd been given. A week in this idyllic, snow-covered place with a man whose love seemed relentless, and whose family represented what she'd dreamed about as a child. And a teen. And yesterday.

Christmas Week, at that. She'd have to apologize to Jesus too.

She leaned her head toward Micah's ear. "When do we start sharing our regrets?"

"We don't share them," he whispered back to her. "We let them go."

It started at the far end of the semicircle around the bonfire. Micah's parents stood. Each picked a foot-long broken branch from a pile separate from the wood that was stacked to keep feeding the fire.

They gripped their branches and pondered, judging by the sober looks on their faces. What could Deb and Tim have to regret? Katie had never heard a cross word between them. Eventually, they tossed the twigs into the heart of the fire and held each other a moment, heads bowed. Katie thought she might have heard them praying.

Titus and Rhonda's girls went next. The eldest, Starburst, held her twig and tapped it on her palm. She turned to her mom and said, "I can't think of anything." Rhonda stepped near her and said something into her ear.

"Oh, yeah," Starburst said. She flung the stick toward the

fire and brushed its dust from her mittened hands. "Done," she said and returned to her log perch.

Her sisters took a little longer, their postures almost comically serious. After they'd added their regrets to the fire, they held hands all the way back to their places. A commitment to less sibling rivalry in the upcoming year?

Uncle Paul took a half-dozen sticks. Allie gave him two more and picked up one of her own. When all the Binders except Micah were done, Katie stood. Micah stood with her, but she motioned for him to let her do this alone.

She walked to the pile, wrapped her arms around the remaining bundle, juggled it in her arms a moment, then tossed the whole thing into the flames. Only she and God would know the names of her regrets. She watched them flare up and turn to ashes more quickly than she'd imagined they could.

Micah picked up the stick she'd left for him and broke it in half. He tossed one into the fire, then turned to his grandparents.

"I have a deep regret. I lied to you."

Everyone under the age of twelve gasped and said, "Ooh!"

"Grandma Dodie, Grandpa Wilson, Mom and Dad, I know it's important to you that we unplug this week, but I snuck my iPad out of the box tonight." He pulled it from the deep pockets of his coat. "I hope you'll forgive me. But we need it so we can Skype with Courtney and Brogan."

Grandma Dodie pressed her hand to her heart. Tim and Deb bolted out of their chairs. The whole crew huddled behind the grandparents, pressing for a view of the screen Micah held like the smallest outdoor theater screen in the world.

"Give me a minute," Micah said, pressing buttons and adjusting the screen brightness and volume. "Courtney, are you there?"

"We're here."

Micah waved Katie closer to the family cluster so she could see too. What a sight! Courtney was as beautiful as her photos, but with a pink glow on her cheeks and a small bundle in her arms. Behind her stood her husband, taller by far than his wife.

"You have the baby?" Grandma Dodie said, clapping her hands together. "Let us see."

Courtney pulled back the receiving blanket to reveal a dark-haired infant. "Meet little Evan Wilson Greene."

The Binders jostled for a better view. Grandpa Wilson's facial expression brought tears to Katie's eyes.

A wild chorus of congratulations must have startled the baby, whose arm escaped the blanket and waved in return.

"Brogan wants to say something too," Courtney said.

Her husband leaned over her shoulder to get closer to their computer's microphone. "I just wanted to thank you all for your input in making this miracle happen. And to say that Courtney and I are so grateful for your love and generosity, and would like you to meet Evan's brother, Gabe."

"What?" Deb grabbed Tim's arm.

Courtney stepped aside to reveal another bundle in Brogan's arms.

"Twins?" Grandma Dodie leaned forward, as if she couldn't believe what she was seeing.

"Hey!" Twilight said.

Titus touched his daughter on her shoulder and said, "Let the adults do the talking first, honey. You'll get a turn."

"But—"

"Twilight . . ."

"But, Daddy, that's Grandma Dodie's Christmas tree in the background."

"So it is," Titus said, smiling. "Merry Christmas, Mom and Dad. Let's go meet those babies close-up."

"They're here?" Grandma Dodie bolted out of her chair with the energy of a teen cheerleader. "Here?"

"Yes, Grandma," Micah said. "They're in the house, waiting for you." He closed the cover of the iPad and took her arm. "Dad, do you have Grandpa?"

"I do."

Micah winked at Katie, who held back while the Binders-by-birth-and-marriage streamed toward the cottage.

So this is what outrageous, extravagant love looks like.

"Don't let her slip on the step!" Wilson moved as fast as he dared, as fast as Tim's firm armhold would allow him, but Dodie had taken off as if she had no ailments and that hip wasn't waiting for a more convenient day for its replacement. That woman was a wonder. What would he do if something happened to her?

Wilson breathed a little easier when he saw Allie and Deb, the brand new grandma, helping Dodie into the house. A little easier. This cold air. Not good for the lungs. He turned when they finally reached the threshold. Katie stayed by the fire.

"Katie? Come on in with us."

"I'll be in after a bit."

"Okay, dear." He thanked Tim for the assistance. "Son!"

"What is it? Do you have pain somewhere?"

"No. It just now occurred to me that we both got new names a minute ago. Congratulations, Grandpa Binder."

Tim laughed. "And congratulations to you, Great-grandpa. Now, let's go meet those name-changers."

"After you." *I need to catch my breath. Great-grandparenting isn't for sissies.*

Great-grandsons. Never thought he'd live to see the day. Or that he'd get two at a once.

CHAPTER EIGHT

THE TWINS GOT A DEEP-DUNK initiation into Binder-style celebrating. And Katie only heard the faint strains of it as the noise leaked out of the house. She stayed behind, watching the fire until it died down to embers, collecting folding chairs and stacking them inside the addition of the horse-less barn. Half of the rec room, with four sets of bunk beds, looked like a girls' dorm at college mashed with a slumber party for preteens. The other half seemed more activity-oriented, with a combo pool table/Ping-Pong table, a crafting center, and a wall of hooks and bins for skates, skis, snowshoes, and fishing equipment.

Katie perspired under her cold weather clothing as she hauled patio furniture through the snow to the apron of concrete on the garage side of the barn. When she finally felt emotionally strong enough to walk into the cottage, she piled abandoned quilts on top of the dryer in the mudroom. Assuming most of them would be needed at bedtime, she'd have to start throwing them into the dryer one at a time to melt off and dry any remnants of snow. One more chore to take care of first. She headed back outside.

How did the family pull off getting Micah's sister and her husband—and two infants—from Korea, across the country, and into the house without the unsuspecting suspecting? She wondered how many knew about the plan. Micah hadn't breathed a word to her. Didn't he trust her?

Paranoia. A regret she'd burned less than an hour ago. Knowing Micah, he probably was as excited to surprise her as he had been to see the look on his grandparents' face.

As if sensing her thoughts, he stuck his head outside to urge her to join the melee.

"Can I just leave the fire?"

"It's surrounded by eight inches of snow. But we'll keep an eye on it through the kitchen window. Come on in. Those babies are—" He pressed both hands over his heart in a gesture that looked so much like how his grandmother would have expressed herself. "Wait. I'd better come out. We'll need embers from the fire."

"For what?"

Micah stepped into his boots, coatless, and grabbed a metal pail and a shovel from near the back door. "We build a fire in the fireplace with embers from our regret fire. I know. We're the sappy family. I told you we weren't for the faint of heart."

Oh, but you are. You're so good for the faint of heart. "How can I help?"

"Nestle the bucket into the snow so it doesn't tip over." Micah dug the shovel blade-deep into the glowing embers. "Stand back, hon."

Had he called her that before?

He slid the embers into the pail and slid the shovel blade through the snow to clean it. "Okay. That's about all the colder I want to get tonight. Let's head inside."

"I could have done that for you."

He faked a pout. "I'm the only grandson. Collecting the embers has been my job since I was twelve years old."

"Correction, Micah. You're now the oldest grandson. There are two others."

"That's going to take some getting used to. But it won't be hard. Nothing like babies to liven up a Christmas party."

"Where are they going to sleep in all that commotion?"

He held the door for her. "Grandma and Grandpa say they have it all figured out. They've given their room to Courtney and Brogan and the boys. Listen to that. The boys."

"Money well spent?"

"Definitely."

Katie removed her coat and boots. She tucked a damp quilt into the dryer and pushed the button to start it. Micah held his pail of burning embers away from his body. "So, where are your grandparents sleeping?" she asked.

Grandma Dodie opened the door between the kitchen and mudroom. "Well, there you are, roommate. We were beginning to think you two had eloped."

"Roommate?" Katie looked from Grandma Dodie to Micah. Neither responded, but the answer was clear when they stepped into the kitchen. The table was gone. In its place lay a two-foot-thick airbed. Allie and Deb were stretching a fitted sheet over its corners.

"Half of us volunteered to give up our spots," Deb said. "Grandma insisted. She said it'll be easier for her to keep an eye on the turkey while it cooks tomorrow. And the ham on Christmas Day."

"I don't have a problem with getting a room in town. Honestly," Katie said, not that freeing her window seat bed would help any.

Grandma Dodie folded her hands in front of her middle. "It's not the same unless we're all here."

That settled it. Katie had roommates.

How many more names was Katie going to have to master before the week was over? Evan and . . . ? Ah. Gabe. Like the angel Gabriel.

"Courtney, Brogan, this is Katie," Micah said when he pulled her toward the huddle of happiness on one of the couches in the family room.

Brogan stretched his hand toward her. "Nice to meet you, Katie. And congratulations are in order, eh?"

Courtney elbowed her husband with her one free arm. "She said no."

"What? You're kidding, right?" His countenance fell. "You're not kidding. Oh, I am so sorry. I apologize profusely, and if it will help, I'll give blood at the next blood drive."

"It's okay," Katie said. "You're no more uncomfortable than I've been for the last two days. Really, it's . . . it's going to be okay. Now, which baby is which?"

"This is Gabe," Courtney said, kissing his little forehead before handing him to Katie. "I feel as if I'm in a dream world."

"A sleepless dream world," Brogan added.

"How were the flights?" Katie traced a finger around the perfectly formed head and downy soft cheeks.

"Long." Both new parents answered at once.

"But the boys slept most of the way," Courtney said. "All three of them."

Brogan stepped away from the women. "Micah, need help getting that fire started?"

Katie sat in the spot Brogan had vacated next to his wife. "Where's Evan?"

"Aunt Allie, Aunt Rhonda, and my mother are changing his diaper. Kind of a circus, isn't it?"

"But you must be loving every minute of it."

"Now we are," Courtney said. "The wait seemed interminable. And having to keep it from my parents and grandparents that we'd been able to finalize everything in time to get here for Christmas was tough. And that we were bringing two boys home, not one. Life got considerably more complicated in the last week."

Katie noted how Gabe fit perfectly in the crook of her arm. The weight of him felt completely natural. Probably from her pediatrics rotation during training. Probably. "So did my life."

"Are you really doing okay? I hadn't had time to tell Brogan."

"I love your brother."

"What's not to love?" Courtney's smile was a female version of Micah's.

"We have some things to work out before— No. That's not accurate. I have some things to work out."

"Kind of hard to think with all this going on, isn't it?"

"It's going to take more than thinking. But, strange as it might sound, I believe this is where I'm supposed to be right now."

"I can trace most of my smartest decisions to this place and this family." Courtney leaned her head back and closed her eyes.

"Seems to be a theme. If you want to sleep for a while, I don't mind taking one watch. I could come and get you when Gabe stirs."

Courtney opened her eyes. "You and I are sitting on someone's bed."

"Oh, that's right."

"I've waited a long time to lose sleep because a child needed me. But ask again in a week or so." She closed her eyes once more. "It's the fire in the fireplace. So relaxing."

Healing.

Gabe's forehead wrinkled. Whatever thoughts galloped through his young mind, he would never have to wonder if he was loved. Interesting. Days ago, he'd been an orphan. The embrace of this family changed all that.

A bubble of air caught in her throat. Orphaned. Embrace of this family. She needed to stop thinking so much.

"What time is it?" Courtney asked, her eyes still closed.

"After ten. All the younger ones have found their nests already."

"Grandma and Grandpa dishing out their evening hugs and blessings still?"

A surge of emotion made her hope they hadn't skipped it tonight. "They're setting up camp in the kitchen."

"Nobody like those two," Courtney said. "Grandpa seems more tired than normal."

So Katie wasn't the only who noticed.

Courtney sighed. "We have to make the most of every moment we have with them."

Gabe opened his mouth as if to make an angelic pronouncement. Katie shifted him to her shoulder. He nestled his forehead against her neck and calmed again. "You heard about Jericho?"

No answer.

No apology would come out right. Katie could hear now the assurance that it hadn't been her fault. The horse had "finished his life," as Grandma Dodie said. No point in apologizing yet again.

And no need. Courtney had fallen asleep.

The adults enjoyed the fire in the family room for a while, those persistent carols playing more softly in the background now that there were babies to consider. "A child, a child, sleeping in the night . . ."

What were the odds they would?

"Silent Night." Probably not.

But plenty of "Joy to the World" anyway.

Grandpa Wilson installed a mini fridge and coffeemaker in the master bedroom the year Grandma Dodie had her first hip replacement, Micah said. As a side benefit, now, in the middle of the night, the new parents could make formula for the babies without having to leave the master. Katie hoped the room had enough space for pacing and rocking. Or maybe these darlings would cut their exhausted parents some slack and . . .

And reindeer really can fly.

Tim and Deb tried one more time to convince Tim's parents to trade the kitchen's airbed for the spare room.

"Twin beds," Grandma Dodie said. "No thank you. I

don't sleep well without being able to reach out in the night and know he's there."

Tim sighed. "Just for a couple of days?"

Deb laid her hand on her husband's shoulder.

Katie took Micah's hand. He squeezed her fingers as if reading her thoughts. How many nights would his grandparents have left to sleep side by side? The conversation on that subject was over. No matter how awkward it would be for them to crawl into a bed that low to the ground.

The blessing routine had long ago been completed for the younger ones. As the fire faded to embers again, the others filed past the matriarch and patriarch to collect their evening hugs and prayers. Katie didn't hesitate this time. She craved those sweet words of benediction for the day and promise for tomorrow. Grandpa Wilson's cheek had felt a little clammy, but that could have been from the fireplace heat and the crowded room.

She'd curled into her window seat, a fresh-from-the-dryer quilt between her and the window, by the time Grandpa Wilson and Grandma Dodie settled onto the airbed.

"Good night, Katie."

"Good night."

"Let's sleep until noon, okay?"

Katie chuckled. "I will if you will, Grandpa Wilson."

"Katie?"

"Yes?"

"We forgot to turn out the light before we got all snuggled in here." Grandma Dodie sounded well on her way to sleep.

"I'll get it." Katie left her snug cocoon and padded across the floor and around the octogenarian campers to the wall switch.

"Thank you."

"You're welcome." She tiptoed back by the thin light of a cloud-shrouded moon.

"Wilson?" Grandma Dodie's voice sounded even nearer the edge of sleep, yet still insistent.

"I didn't forget."

Katie heard the airbed shift and an almost breathless baritone version of the first verse of "Amazing Grace."

SHE MISSED THE foot warmer she'd had the night before. Tired as she was, it seemed obvious it would take her even longer to fall asleep tonight.

The night before Christmas Eve millennia ago. Christmas Eve Eve, Micah called it. Shepherds minding their own business. Angels on high alert. Wise men scanning the skies, not yet aware they'd see a new star the next night. Mary . . .

Mary probably wishing she had something as luxurious as a cozy window seat in a sweet cottage, crowded with family. Joseph as concerned as Courtney's Brogan about what the upcoming days and years would look like.

A muffled cry sounded from somewhere deep in the

darkened cottage. She smiled. The parents had probably only been in bed a half hour.

As another small voice joined the first cry, Katie turned over, her back against the window quilt. The makeshift bed felt wider than it had before. And emptier. Maybe it was because of the couple devoted to each other for six decades, lying on their own makeshift bed a few feet away, holding hands as they slept.

She adjusted her pillows. It was her thoughts she couldn't adjust. They tried to retrieve regrets from a long burned-out fire.

Her earplugs were two rooms away, buried somewhere in her luggage in the front closet. Her ear buds and phone lay in a box of forbidden technology for the week. No music would drown out the noise of her wandering mind. If she were home, she would have turned on the television to watch a mind-numbing movie. If she were home.

In some ways, in this curious environment with no real room in the inn, she felt more at home than she ever had.

Holding on to it longer than a few more days was the problem.

By the moon's faint nightlight, Katie could read the wall clock. Three in the morning. She'd fallen asleep sometime, against all odds. What woke her now?

"Wilson. Wilson?"

"What is it?"

"Shh. You'll wake our Katie."

"What do you need, love?"

"Would you help me with my leg? I want to roll over."

Faint as it was, Katie heard the sound of a tender kiss. "Certainly."

Within moments, she heard, "Thank you, sweet man."

"You're welcome, sweet woman."

Then the soft sounds of almost-snoring. Comfortable and comforted, they'd drifted back to sleep without effort, it seemed.

On a couch in the family room was a man who'd gotten down on one knee and volunteered to be Katie's Wilson, to be woken in the middle of the night when sixty years from now she needed help turning over in bed.

And she'd said no.

Katie already had a regret for next year's bonfire.

December twenty-fourth dawned with Katie still searching for a peace-on-earth thought that would override her soul-crushing debt and—rational or not—her relationship-challenged genes.

She tiptoed around her still sleeping hosts and stealthed her way through the family room and down the hall to the bathroom, which was, understandably so, vacant at dawn. She showered with the water barely trickling through the showerhead so as not to wake the household prematurely. Her hair would have to air-dry today.

Dressed in the clothes she'd squirreled away in the narrow linen closet behind the bathroom door, she turned off the light before opening the door. She stood in the hall a moment, letting her eyes adjust to the half-light. The recessed bookcase directly in front of her held photos and photo albums. She stepped closer to read the labels on the spines of the albums.

"Christmas Past" caught her eye. Would they mind if she . . . ?

She slid the album from its perch as noiselessly as possible and held it against her chest as she retraced her steps to the kitchen. Still not enough light there. She padded into the mudroom, laid yesterday's clothes along the crack at the bottom of the door, and flicked the light switch.

The hard bench in the mudroom needed a thick cushion like her window seat. She grabbed a spare quilt that had had its turn in the dryer but wasn't needed at bedtime. Wrapped in it, burrito-style, she sat on the bench and opened the photo album.

What year had the Binders abandoned the tradition of dressing alike for their annual Christmas photo? Not just all denim or all red. Several of the pictures showed the family in matching shirts, matching sweatshirts, matching pajamas. Sometime after the Binder boys married, the tradition ceased.

Katie held the album closer when she saw a younger version of Micah's parents, each holding a toddler. She probably would have fallen in love with Micah in the nursery at church if she'd known him then, with those piercing, pale-blue eyes and that unchanged full-faced smile. Without even knowing that inside him beat a heart two sizes too big.

She turned the stiff pages slowly. Years of Christmases with just Micah and Courtney until Bella and Elisa eventually doubled the number of grandchildren. She laid her hand on the photo of Silas and a woman with dark circles under her eyes, a familiar hollowness at the base of her neck. Lynda. Mackenzie and Madeline's mom. A note on the white border of the photo read, "Never know when it may be our last together."

Is that when it started? With Lynda's illness? Is that when the Binders started cherishing every moment as if it might be the last?

No, she'd seen similar phrases earlier in the album. Randomly scattered. A river of thought that ran underground, then surfaced, then dove underground again.

Christmas 2011. A whole page of photos. Micah with his arm draped around a woman Katie didn't recognize. Micah and said woman in the sleigh. Micah and the designer coiffed woman sitting side by side, their faces lit by the bonfire.

"She said yes!" the caption read.

Katie's stomach soured. She should have grabbed a banana on her way through the kitchen. She didn't do well in the mornings on an empty stomach. Or an empty heart.

Micah assured her he'd never proposed to any of his previous girlfriends. Not that it would have mattered, but she expected him to be honest with her. She trusted him to be honest. She'd said yes. And no matter where that woman was now, the truth was that Micah had lied to her after all.

The sleepless night trying to figure out how she could stay with him? Wasted. She couldn't deal with dishonesty. She had enough of that maneuvering through her parents' anything-but-amicable divorce.

The decision had been made for her. No matter why Micah and Ms. Perfection hadn't followed through with their wedding, Katie now had more than enough solid reasons why it could never work out between them.

She should have felt relief to finally have a definitive answer. The tears burning her sinuses didn't feel at all like relief.

"Katie? Is that you in there?" Grandma Dodie sounded concerned.

She swiped at her eyes. "I was . . . reading. Didn't want to disturb you."

"Take your time. But you should know, dear, there's a bra strap sticking out from under the door."

It wasn't hard to avoid Micah at breakfast. With even more mouths to feed, the family ate in shifts. First ready, first fed. Grandma Dodie insisted they couldn't afford to have the men do the cleanup, despite the new snow that again reached an odd number on her yardstick. She shooed everyone but a skeleton crew out of the kitchen so she could get the prep work done for the Christmas Eve turkey dinner. The Christmas hams for the following day were thawing in the refrigerator in the barn addition.

A side effect of sleeping in the kitchen would mean the airbed would have to be dismantled every morning and the table hauled back in from wherever it was the men had stored it. For Katie, the chief side effect was heightened lack of privacy. Alone hadn't appealed to her this strongly until shortly after dawn. Now it ate at her like an addict's craving.

She'd replaced the photo album, but tucked the one Polaroid print into her jean jacket pocket. When the time came to confront, she'd need evidence.

Bella and Elisa volunteered to keep the younger girls busy with crafts in the rec room for the morning, hinting that they were working on something related to the family Christmas Eve celebration. The men headed for the pond ice and their epic broom hockey tournament. Their raised voices drifted to the cottage over each point scored or each near-miss. Micah's voice, always calming before, stabbed at her like the handle end of his broom. Integrity was his calling card. Even when he was a little too laid-back for the situation at hand, she could always count on his honesty. Before.

The air of joy in the kitchen rivaled the delicious aromas of pies baking and cranberry-sage dressing. It would be hours before the turkeys added their unique fragrance. But the women, dovetailing their skills, dodging each other expertly as they worked, gave off an almost tangible exuberance, as if each knife cut, each egg broken, each stir of spoon or whisk had its genesis in love for the family that would sit down to that meal at day's end.

"Are you feeling all right, Katie?"

Deb's perception rattled her. "I didn't sleep well last night." Truth. Not the whole truth.

"Oh, that was probably our fault," Grandma Dodie said, removing a pecan pie from the top rack of the oven and setting it to cool on an unoccupied cutting board. "Wilson and I compete for decibel levels snoring."

"No. It wasn't that."

"Well, let's hope the turkey tryptophan rocks you to sleep tonight, Katie."

"Melatonin is more reliable," Rhonda said. "All natural. I have a supply, if you need some. And if you rub a good quality lavender oil on your feet, that will help too. You let me know if you want some for tonight."

"I will. Thank you."

"I have a suggestion for Katie." Courtney stood in the doorway to the kitchen, her hair wrapped in a towel, which reminded Katie she needed to dig out her curling wand later.

"Courtney. You got a shower!" Deb held her floured hands out to the side and kissed her daughter on the cheek. "I was going to offer to watch the boys for you so you could."

"Brogan begged off the first round of the broom hockey tourney. I promised he could take a nap if he let me shower first."

"He's a good man," Grandma Dodie said.

She'd said that about Micah too.

"My suggestion," Courtney said, snatching a matchstick carrot from the relish tray work of art Allie was preparing, "is a cup of strong coffee, like they make at the Daily Grind in Stillwater."

"We have coffee here," Deb said, nodding toward the rarely inactive coffeemaker.

"S-t-r-o-n-g coffee." Courtney held out two twenty-dollar bills. "It appears the new parents grossly underestimated the number of diapers twins could go through in a day. We'll need more by tomorrow, and nothing will be open on Christmas Day. I'm looking for someone willing to go to town for us and thought it would be a great opportunity for Micah and Katie to have some alone time. Granted, it's only five miles each direction, but—"

"Great idea," Allie said. "After the way their sleigh ride ended, I'm sure they'd appreciate time to wish each other a merry Christmas without twenty other people around." She smiled at Katie. "Take your time at the coffee shop. We've got this covered."

Katie's temples pounded. Lack of sleep could do that. Lack of caffeine. Loss.

"Micah's—"

"Right behind you." His arms encircled her and he planted a kiss on her cheek.

"Your nose is an icicle!" She pulled away, matching her facial expression to the fake disgust the watching women expected her to project. "What happened to hockey?"

"Trounced them. And we're down one broom. I was nominated to go to town for spares for this afternoon's and tomorrow's matches."

The Binder women laughed at the timing.

"There you go, Katie. Turn in your virtual apron." Courtney handed her the twenties and a coupon for their preferred brand of disposable diapers. "Get two of the largest packages they have, if that's enough money after you take out the coffee."

"Coffee, brooms, diapers . . . Anything else?" Micah asked.

"We'll need chamomile tea for Katie tonight," Rhonda said.

"What for?"

"Never mind, Micah. I'll get my coat," Katie said.

"I love your hair like that," he said as they exited through the mudroom.

"Very funny."

"I'm serious. All tousled on top of your head."

Katie grabbed the hat Grandma Binder had made for her and crammed it over her untamed curls. "We'd better get going."

"Yes, ma'am." Micah held the door for her as they headed for the rental car lined up with the others behind the barn.

No, no, no. This was the kind of tension she'd felt every Christmas of her childhood. This was not how she envisioned confronting Micah, in anger. She was more mature than that.

They would talk, but she'd keep her composure. And her hand on the photo in her pocket.

It was going to be one of those days, Wilson thought. His best bet was to stay out of the way. His sons could ably handle the details he would have taken care of in his younger days. No shame in that, right? And if he managed to sneak in an extra nap, what would that hurt?

He'd have to ask one of the boys to get some WD40 for the footrest handle of his recliner. It seemed stiffer than ever. Aw, he didn't need his feet up this time.

He didn't like telling Titus and Rhonda's girls and Silas's two that he didn't feel up to doing his "Rindercella" routine today. Some other day, he'd told them. Not like him. Passing up an opportunity to make those little girls giggle? Not like him at all.

Maybe it was time to pass on the tradition to one of the other Binder men. And reciting the Christmas story? Last year he'd stumbled. This year how much of it would he remember without prompts from the young girls?

He could turn the job over to them. They knew the story as well as he did, if not better.

Not a tradition he relished giving up. He took such joy in watching each face react to the words, watching the over-achievers mouthing the words with him, or blurting them out if he paused for a breath.

How did it start? He should know this. His Bible sat on the end table inches away. Nice large print, but that made it heavy as a sack of horse feed.

Jericho, old boy, you gave your all, didn't you?

Animals. Flocks. That was it. And there were in the same country shepherds abiding in the fields, keeping watch over their flocks by night. And lo . . .

And lo . . . ?

CHAPTER NINE

"WILD DAY YESTERDAY, WASN'T IT?" Micah said shortly after he and Katie left the Binders' driveway on their mission to find diapers.

"Wild."

"I think everyone was genuinely surprised when Courtney and Brogan showed up with the little ones."

"Shocked."

"I would have let you in on it," Micah said, "but, I guess selfishly, I wanted it to be a surprise for you too."

"It was."

"I knew you and Courtney would hit it off. And I'm doing all the talking. Do you want to pick up our conversation where we left it when Jericho—"

"It's a moot point now." Katie leaned her head on the side window, then sat upright when she realized that's how their trip from the airport to Stillwater had started. With her uncertain and vulnerable. No more. Strength was her ally. Her nemesis was the fact she still admired him, appreciated him, and okay, loved him, and she cringed at the idea of having to live without him.

But strong women don't make excuses for men who lie.

The side road was no easier to navigate than it had been when they arrived. She couldn't show him the photo yet. She'd have to hold it together until they could sit across from one another. The strong cup of coffee sounded better and better.

"So," she said, the ache in her chest growing, "what's Christmas Eve like with the Binders?" The general atmosphere, she could guess.

"One of my favorite nights all year. The meal's spectacular, as you can imagine. There's a candlelight service at a little country church not far from us. It's not our home church, but it's kind of amazing to have our family fill most of the pews in the tiny building. Tradition."

"A lot of that going around."

"Then we come home and make a fire in the fireplace and paint each other's toenails."

"You're not serious!"

Micah laughed, the sound filling the car and somehow reaching to her soul. "Just seeing if you were paying attention," he said. "I haven't seen you smile all day." He turned onto the main highway toward Stillwater.

She removed the knit cap, pulled down the car's visor, and fluffed her hair in the mirror. Maybe it wasn't so bad.

"I think you're going to have to learn to live with it, Katie."

"My hair?"

"Your debt."

"What?"

Micah slowed to avoid the overspray of a snowplow ahead. "Not live with it permanently, of course. You're already working on it. But I think you're letting it control how you feel about . . . about our potential together."

That was yesterday.

"Love takes on other people's debts, Katie. That's kind of the point of Christmas, don't you think?"

Katie sensed one small muscle relaxing at the top of her shoulder blades. At his core, he hadn't changed. Logic pressed its nose against the glass of her doubts about him. "You do know Christmas is about the birth of the Christ-child, Savior of the world, not the birth of a financial planner."

"Actually, He can do both, but that's beside the point. He came to remove the debt from our shoulders and carry it on His own. Why would you think a) that a real estate purchase that didn't work out would be an unforgiveable sin and b) that love wouldn't be enough to compel me to help bear your debt in order to spend the rest of my life with you?"

The conversation had derailed at the intersection. If she didn't get it back on track . . .

"Coffee first?" he asked.

"Probably a good idea." Determination sat in her jacket pocket. It needed fortification.

"Daily Grind?" Katie thought of all the cute coffee shop names she'd seen in the last ten years. Four or five Daily Grinds. None had a view like this one. The river, the lift bridge, the frosted hills on the other side . . . live music. Nice touch. Victorian carolers in full costume. They made the wait for the specialty coffee more than worth it.

"White chocolate mocha with nutmeg." Micah set her drink in front of her.

"Did you get your traditional latte?"

"You know the Binders. We love shaking up tradition once in a while. I got a Frozen River."

Katie eyed his mystery beverage.

"Coffee slush. Want a taste?"

"Cold coffee on a day like today?"

Micah moved the small Christmas decoration from the center of their round table to the side and reached for her hand. "You know what they say: cold coffee, warm heart."

She didn't take his hand.

"Okay. I deserved that," he said. "I told you I wouldn't push you. But I've done a lot of talking aimed at defusing your fears."

She bristled.

"Not fears," he said. "No. Resistance?"

Her bristles formed bristles.

"Katie"—he linked his fingers behind his neck—"I know these concerns are very real to you."

"To me?" She sipped her mocha. It scalded her tongue like his words scalded her soul. "Did you bring me here to point out my weak spots?"

"No." He seemed shocked. "Your strong places."

She stared out the window, her jaw flirting with TMJ.

"This isn't going well," he said. "Can we call a Christmas truce, like they do in . . . in . . . ?"

"World wars?"

His expression was the blue-eyed version of a penitent cocker spaniel. She reached into her pocket and slid the photo across the table. When his eyes widened but he failed to say anything, she pointed to the neat lettering on the white margin: She said yes!

"Where did you find this?"

"Photo album in the hall. Don't expect me to apologize for snooping. It was in a public place. Not hidden, as one might assume." She amazed herself at her level, unembittered tone. Had she finally resigned herself to the only right decision?

He picked up the image and held it with a tenderness that ripped through her.

"I didn't know Grandma Dodie still had any of these pictures around. That's . . . wow."

Katie clasped her hands in her lap to keep them from shaking. "You told me you'd never proposed to anyone but me."

"Katie—"

"It's not the proposing that matters to me. It's that you lied. I don't know that you've ever lied to me before. But now I have to wonder, as you can imagine." She didn't like the harsh edge that now crept into her voice. But she had no energy to correct it.

He laid the Polaroid on the table and slid it toward her. She didn't touch it.

"Susie was . . ."

"Your fiancée." Why would Katie have to coach him on that word?

"No." He continued to stare at the photo.

"Micah, she"—Katie pointed to the individual words—"said yes."

He lifted his eyes. "Not to marriage. To Jesus." He swirled the slush in his drink. "I'd never had a best friend who proclaimed to be an atheist before I met Susie in college. We were in a lot of the same classes our junior year. History geeks. I think I might have been the first Jesus person who wanted to know how she thought, how she came to her conclusions. We had some interesting conversations those two years."

"And then you fell in love."

"Friend love. Sister love. Compassion kind of love."

"I keep telling myself the only thing that matters is that I thought you'd been dishonest with me. It isn't jealousy. No. Couldn't be that," Katie said. "We've both been attracted to other people in the past. But you'd never told me about this 'her.' And the look on your face in this picture is— What woman wouldn't want to have someone feel that way about her?"

"I wasn't trying to keep her from you, Katie."

An edge of defensiveness in his response raised the hairs on Katie's forearms.

He stared at the Polaroid again. "The subject never came up."

"And that doesn't sound at all like something a guy would say when trying to hide a past relationship? Look at the expression on your face in that picture. You obviously care deeply about her."

"Like I said, as a friend . . ."

"A 'friend' you invited to your grandparents' for Christmas."

Micah curled the corner of the napkin resting under his drink. "I have a theory. I didn't always think this, but listening, really listening to Susie during those long discussions made me consider what I'd been missing before."

His calmness disarmed her. It always did. "Go on."

"Change one letter in atheist, move it over a spot, and you can form the word athirst. Susie said she didn't believe God exists, but at her core, she thirsted for Him. It took a lot of listening for me to figure that out. No, that's wrong. For her to figure it out. My faith grew more during those two years than I can ever explain. She made me examine why I believed what I did, not just parrot what I'd heard from other people."

Katie leaned back in her chair. *You did that for me a few weeks after we met.*

"I invited Susie to the cottage for Christmas," Micah said, "because she needed a place and a time where the pieces would all come together for her. Away from school. I wanted her to talk to Courtney."

"Courtney?"

"Courtney wrestled with some of the same issues in her high school years."

That the perfect Binder family had "wrestled" with anything close to that kind of issue unclenched nerve endings around her heart.

"It wasn't even at the candlelight service or when Grandpa Wilson recited the Christmas story from the book of Luke or when we prayed together as a family. No." Micah looked out across the icy river. "She couldn't get over what she called the 'sustainability' of our joy. At the bonfire she announced that she'd burned her last regret and intended to celebrate a perpetual Christmas every day for the rest of her life. An endless Christmas."

"I can imagine how the family reacted."

He turned to face Katie again and tapped the photo. "Like I did."

Micah retrieved his wallet from his back pocket. Hadn't he paid before picking up the coffees? He slid a small piece of paper from a plastic compartment and unfolded it. "I'd show you on my phone if Grandma hadn't confiscated it." Did his small smile mean the tension between them could let up a little?

"It's us." Katie looked at the photocopied image of the two of them standing ankle-deep in the Gulf of Mexico. It looked like the beach at Bradenton.

He flipped the photo from the Christmas album around so both pictures faced her. "Which one looks like a man happy for his friend and which one looks like a man happy because he's deliriously in love?"

She hesitated, captivated by what she saw. "I pick this one." She held the beach picture.

Micah didn't play the role of debate victor. If anything, he looked more sober than ever.

"Why do you put up with my doubts about myself . . . or about you?" Katie asked. "And just so you know, I'm officially apologizing for misreading this latest one." She cupped her hands around the still-too-hot-to-drink coffee container. And please don't say, "I'm wondering the same thing."

"I got a crash course in patience from Susie. Maybe that was the wrong illustration. I only meant that she might never have found what she was thirsting for if I'd rushed her through the thought process that eventually brought her to that beautiful conclusion."

"So, I'm your next project?"

"You're the love of my life. I think you're trying to tell yourself that's not possible. The stories and reasons and pursuits are completely different, but that's where Susie stayed for a long time. Once she began to entertain the idea that God existed, she fought the concept that He found her lovable, redeemable."

"Are history teachers always this insightful and relational? I thought they were more facts-oriented." Katie placed the photo back into her pocket and reached across the table toward him.

"I'm not a history teacher."

"Not yet." Her comment netted a sigh that ended with his kiss on the back of her hand.

"Christmas truce, then?" He didn't let go of her hand while waiting for an answer.

"Truce."

"I need a hug," he said.

"Me too."

"Let's go get diapers."

"Because that's perfectly logical and linear thinking." She laughed.

"Perfectly. Hug. Huggies. The babies need diapers. We'd better get back before they think we eloped."

For a fraction of a second, eloping sounded perfectly logical and linear.

They exited the Daily Grind arm in arm, which turned into a quick hug—nowhere near the twenty seconds necessary to release enough naturally occurring oxytocin to make Katie trust Micah more. When she read about the hug-length connection on the Internet, it confirmed what she'd learned in nursing school. She hoped to add practical anecdotal evidence to support the claim.

Micah opened the passenger door of the rental car for Katie. She'd have to trust him more not because of the length of a hug, but because it made sense.

"How far is the store?"

"Grandma and Grandpa much prefer a quaint corner grocery store a few blocks off Main Street."

"I know," she said. "We stopped there yesterday for milk."

"But with the volume of diapers we need, I think we'd better head to the SuperStore. It's out by the high school. Eight or ten minutes. Maybe a little more with this traffic. Why don't people stay home on Christmas Eve?"

"We didn't."

"Point taken. Let's weave through the back way. You'll see more of the town and we'll miss some of the day crowd from the Cities. The big Victorians and Queen Annes in the residential area are impressive. A lot of them are bed-and-breakfasts. Stillwater's a big wedding destination town, if you hadn't noticed. You'll love the view of the church steeples from the higher elevation. You haven't seen the historic Stillwater Steps yet."

"Rhonda mentioned them."

"Five sets of them built into the steep hills. Have you seen the Lowell Inn?"

"We were going to go there yesterday, but ran out of time. Or was that the place where we needed reservations?"

"I love a town with history in it."

Maybe that helped explain his interest in her. And he hadn't even seen the full report on her mangled family history. He'd asked. Was she ready for that kind of vulnerability yet? A post-grad student could create a compelling dissertation out of a family line that found it impossible to make marriage work. Katie pushed the thought aside. She couldn't afford to let her thoughts drift there. Not if she intended to keep their makeshift Christmas truce, as promised.

The eight or ten minutes to get to the SuperStore turned into considerably more with a sightseeing guide behind the wheel. But they eventually filled the backseat of the small car with infant waste management aids and three brooms and made their way back through town toward the cottage. Katie could almost smell the roast turkey. They'd skipped lunch. But she was sure there were leftovers of some kind that could tide them over until the evening meal.

"Tell me the story about your grandmother measuring the snow depth," she said as Micah turned off of the highway onto Lubber's Lane.

"Family joke. Years ago, Grandma Dodie decided she was tired of the women doing all the cleanup after meals. So she said we'd go by snowfall depth. She'd use a measuring stick to see what the snow total was. Anything closest to an odd number meant the men cleaned up. Closest to an even number of inches meant it was the women's turn."

"I heard that part. You men are mighty unlucky. It seems as if it's been an odd number a lot this week."

"Grandma has two yardsticks. She sawed off the first inch on one of them."

"Does she know you know that?"

"Laughs about it. But still goes through the routine. Years with no snow cover create a problem for her."

"How often does that happen up here?"

"Not often."

"And no one complains?" No, not that family. "Micah?" He'd leaned toward the steering wheel, gripping it hard.

"Katie, do you see lights behind the cottage? Flashing lights?"

The ambulance had backed up to the door. Micah careened around it and parked between the cottage and the barn.

"What happened?" Micah asked his uncle Paul, who brandished a snow shovel and was running toward the front of the house.

"They have to bring him out through the front entrance. Grab a shovel! We'll clear a path for the gurney."

Micah's dad caught up and handed Micah a spare snow shovel. "Dad's unresponsive. Don't know what happened. Just pray."

Katie didn't wait to be told. Micah had left the keys in the car. She pulled it behind the barn when the ambulance driver needed the space to swing around to face the lane. She grabbed the keys and made her way around the barn and to the now-vacated back door. She'd forgotten the diapers in the car. She headed for the commotion, aware of how quickly one critical need could overtake another.

The Binder women clustered around Grandma Dodie at the far end of the family room. Near the fireplace, paramedics worked on Grandpa Wilson, flat on the floor, colorless, unmoving.

Katie put her arm around the nearest Binder woman—Deb. "What happened?"

"Nobody knows. We were all in the kitchen. The men were in the rec room playing pool with the kids."

"The boys and I were napping," Courtney said. "I thought he was too. I didn't hear anything."

"Grandma was peeling potatoes." Allie rubbed the back of Grandma Dodie's shoulders as she talked. The older woman rocked slightly, one hand over her mouth, the other arm angled across her chest. Soft kitten-mewing sobs marked her breaths.

A paramedic looked up at the women. "Can we get a list of his medications?"

"Cabinet to the right of the sink," Grandma Dodie squeezed out.

Katie bolted for the kitchen. "I'll get them. I'm a nurse practitioner." *As if it takes a professional to retrieve a handful of prescriptions. Good grief. It's true what they say—you think you'll be the calm one because of your medical training, until it's someone close to you.*

She expected to have to sort between Grandma Dodie's and Grandpa Wilson's prescription bottles, but each of them had a small zippered plastic bag. Marked. She grabbed his and glanced at the names on the bottles as she flew back to the scene.

Katie rattled off the names of the prescriptions, then called back to Grandma Dodie, "Did he take any vitamins or herbal supplements? Anything other than these prescriptions?"

Rhonda shook her head. She must have suggested a few home remedies that were refused in the past.

Grandma leaned forward, "No. I—" Her words caught on the way out. "I told him, at this age, there was no point in taking Geritol anymore." The sentence brought on tears that had probably been brewing since the family found him unconscious.

She had plenty of comforters. Katie hovered in the space between the women and the paramedics, far enough out of their way to let them do what they did best, but close enough to assist if needed.

"Katie?" Grandma Dodie called to her, her voice little more than a whisper.

She kept the activity in her peripheral vision but bent down to Micah's grandmother. "What?"

"What are they doing?"

"All the right things," Katie said, her longing to ease this time for all of them so strong it threatened to suffocate her. She drew a measured breath. "They're checking and rechecking his vitals, getting him as stable as possible for transfer to the hospital. They have a routine, and it's all purposeful." She reached down to grasp Grandma Dodie's hand. "They're moving as fast as they can and treating him with the respect he deserves."

"Is he . . . awake?"

Katie glanced away, swallowing her own tears. "No. But he's breathing on his own. They have oxygen started, but he's breathing. The oxygen will help him."

One baby, then another started crying in the room down the hall. Life coming and going.

Courtney stood from where she'd been sitting on the floor at Grandma Dodie's feet. She hugged her grandmother and skirted around the paramedics to get to her children. Deb followed her. "She might need help."

"Do the younger girls know?" Katie asked.

Allie said, "Tim told Bella and Elisa to hold the fort in the barn addition until we came to get them. Brogan went out there a few minutes ago to entertain them with his juggling."

Juggling. Circus. The lights from the Christmas tree threw curious patterns on the faces of the two men and one woman bent over Grandpa, now Great-grandpa Wilson. And in the background? Christmas music. Katie inched toward the paramedics. "Anything I can tell the family?"

"I thought you were family," the female said.

"Almost. Practically. He's my . . . my pre-fiancé's grandfather." She'd regret that choice of words in the middle of the night.

The woman raised one eyebrow, then said, "Transporting now." The paramedics raised the transport gurney to its full height and locked it into place. "Tell his wife she can meet us at the hospital," the man said, then lowered his voice further. "Don't have her follow the ambulance. We'll be moving at a pretty good clip. That can be hard on loved ones."

"Understood. Thank you. Can his wife give him a kiss?"

The paramedic nodded. "But only her. We have to move."

"Grandma Dodie? Do you want to tell him you love him and give him a kiss before they take off for the hospital?"

"Make it quick, ma'am," the female paramedic said. "The doctors are waiting for him."

Grandma Dodie leaned in and kissed him on the top of his head. "I'll kiss him full on the lips when he comes through this," she announced.

The medical professionals exchanged a glance Katie hoped Grandma Dodie hadn't seen.

With the path finished, wider and cleaner than it needed to be, the Binder men lined the walk like . . . like pallbearers as the gurney passed by them. Pallbearers leaning on snow shovels.

"We're praying, Grandpa."

"You're in good hands, Dad."

"See you a little bit later."

"God's got this."

"Merry Christmas."

Tim turned to his son. "Micah!"

"I didn't know what to say. That's what came out."

Within minutes the ambulance left the driveway, lights flashing, but no siren. Katie calculated they wouldn't start the siren until the intersection with the highway. The way longer than twenty-second hug from Micah was the most aching embrace she'd known. "It's going to be okay," she whispered.

"Still hurts," he said.

"Not going to argue that."

CHAPTER TEN

FIGURING OUT WHO WOULD DRIVE, who would ride with whom, and when, got more complicated after Grandma Dodie's four sons tried to whisk her away. She tried shouting kitchen commands as her sons held her coat for her, but then stopped. "You women know what to do, don't you?"

"We do," Deb said. "Go be with him."

"You'll come as soon as you can?"

"We'll all come, Mom," Allie added.

The impact of Allie's words hit them when Courtney started to cry. She held a baby in each arm. She wasn't going anywhere. And an emergency room waiting room was no place for five girls fourteen and under. Or three, twelve and under.

Katie was the outsider. Her mind swirled with the complication of tending two small infants and five little girls by herself. But if that's what it took so the older grandchildren and the Binder women could be there for Grandma Dodie and Grandpa Wilson, that's what she'd do.

"Courtney, I don't know if you'd trust me with your little ones, but I can stay here so you can go. And if Aurora and

Twilight and Sunburst and Madeline and MacKenzie"—had she'd remembered them all?—"stay here in the house, I think I can hold things together so the rest of you can be where you need to be."

Micah looked up from the bin in which he was digging for cell phones. She caught the look that told her he'd rather she was with him at the hospital. She mouthed, "Me too."

"Mom, is this yours?" He held up a phone in a basic black case. "Under the circumstances, I think the moratorium on technology is null and void. We're going to need these phones to communicate."

"Agreed," Deb said. "Chargers?"

"That other bin. Labeled this year."

"Smart, son. Thanks."

"Must have been someone else's idea." He glanced at Katie. "We were the last to arrive."

Even in the distress of the moment, Katie's thoughts reverted to that awkwardest of moments. She'd said no.

Brogan hobbled in from outside, pain tattooed across his face.

"What happened to you?" The question came from all corners.

"Juggling incident," he said. "No little girls were injured in the performance of that trick. Ooh!" He hobbled to the nearest chair. "How's Grandpa Wilson?"

"We don't know anything more," Katie said. "I hoped it would be something simple."

Courtney handed Evan and Gabe to two of the nearest Binder women and rushed to her husband.

"It's okay, Courtney. I just need to put my foot up for a while. Don't worry about me, please."

She removed his shoe and sock. "Oh, Brogan! That looks nasty. Katie? Help?"

Katie slipped from child-care thinking back into medical mode and assessed Brogan's injury.

"The girls thought it was part of the act," he said. "There's a rubber ball under the pool table that now has a contract out on its life. Oh. I'm sorry. Bad choice of words."

"Can you put any weight on it?" Katie asked as she felt for bones where they shouldn't be and evaluated the swelling. Two ankles in two days? Really? It wasn't appropriate or within privacy laws to follow up on the woman who'd slipped in front of LoLo's. But she couldn't help wondering. And Grandpa Wilson! *Too much, Lord. Too much.*

"I can put a little weight on it." The creases between Brogan's eyes deepened.

"That's a good sign." Katie patted his knee as she would if he were a four-year-old in need of comfort.

"Ow!"

"Sorry." She waited for him to tell her he was only kidding, but he didn't. He wasn't. "What's up with your knee, Brogan?"

"Kind of twisted it, too, as I fell."

If he called himself Anna, Katie was going to scream.

Courtney started to cry again. "Don't mind me," she said, fanning her face with her hand. "Postpartum hormones."

"Honey, we adopted."

"I'm still entitled!" she said, taking the tissue Micah handed her.

Why was it that crises rarely showed up single? They always seemed to have a mate. Brogan's problems were nowhere near as serious as Grandpa Wilson's, but still needed attention. His right knee looked considerably larger than his left. She palpated gently this time. Lots of swelling. "Do you have any sweatpants or pajama bottoms you could wear for now? You're going to want to get out of those jeans before your knee won't let you."

"I'll get them," Courtney said, sniffing.

"Some of us really should get to the hospital." Allie rubbed her hands as if she'd just applied lotion. "I'm going to ask my girls to stay here and help out. Ellie hates hospitals anyway. Loves her grandpa. Hates hospitals." She grabbed her phone and Ellie's. "I'll run out and tell the girls what's happening while the rest of you decide who'll ride with me."

She got as far as the kitchen and groaned. "We have all this food to take care of."

"I'll get started on that," Rhonda said. She handed Gabe to Deb, who now had both of her grandsons in her arms and a heart likely divided by joy and pain.

"Micah, I think somebody is going to have to take Brogan to the emergency room. I won't feel comfortable about this knee and ankle until they get checked out. Judging by your facial expression, Brogan, I'd guess your pain level is creeping higher."

"I'll wait until we know what's happening with Grandpa Wilson. We don't need another layer of complication right now." Brogan groaned as he adjusted his position in the recliner.

Katie pulled at the elastic holding her hair on top of her head. It didn't help her think more clearly. "If your knee gets any worse, won't that make things even more complicated? What if Micah—the 'muscles' to get you in and out of the car—and Courtney both drove you to the ER? Then Micah can stay with Grandma Dodie and the uncles, and Courtney can drive you back home. She'll get you settled here with the pain meds I'm pretty confident you're going to need, and then she can go back to the hospital. I'll hold down the fort here with the help of Allie's girls."

Courtney returned with flannel pajama bottoms in Christmas red with white faux-ermine on the leg hems.

"Ho, ho, ho, brother-in-law." Micah held his belly.

"We thought the attire would be just between us," Brogan said, wincing. "Do I have to wear those to see the doctor?"

"Your only choice, husband. Everything else we traveled with is in the laundry bag. Tough it out. You picked them."

Somebody was going to have to scream to let off steam over the absurdity of it all. Evan volunteered.

Rhonda called from the kitchen, the sound a curious mix of organic drill sergeant. "Courtney, Katie, come here."

Courtney tossed the Santa Claus pajamas to Micah and said, "Help the poor man while I see what Rhonda wants. Mom, give me Evan."

Katie and Courtney showed up in the kitchen doorway as ordered, Evan content on his mom's shoulder.

"Here's the deal. Courtney, as a mom, you'll find yourself in pickles like this for the rest of your life. Torn between the needs of your children, your husband, and some other family member or cause. Who needs you the most right now?"

Courtney leaned her head against the dark-haired child. "My boys."

"Decision made. You'll stay here with your boys. Katie, you and Micah take Brogan in. Allie and Deb and I will go make sure Grandma Dodie knows we're here for her. We'll talk to Grandpa if we can. Then we'll take shifts coming back here to help out if they keep Grandpa overnight."

Katie didn't want to voice her opinion about how sure she was he would either be there in the hospital overnight or somewhere other than the cottage.

"Your husband will be well cared for," Rhonda said. "Grandma Dodie already knows you have two little ones who went from abandoned to well-loved when you stepped in. Taking you away from them now isn't going to help their transition."

"You're right. An easier choice, when you put it that way."

Rhonda set the timer on the oven. "When that timer goes off, whoever is here, take those turkeys out of the oven. One of us will deal with them when they've cooled off. I put the potatoes in the refrigerator. Nothing else is critical. Let's get this plan implemented."

She reached into the freezer and pulled out two bags of frozen peas. Katie knew what to do with them. She laid one on Brogan's red flannel knee and another on his white fluffy ermine ankle.

Katie grabbed her own cell phone and charger, her coat, gloves, and "Katie" hat, and helped Brogan into his jacket while Micah brought the rental car to the front of the house. They'd take Brogan across the same path Grandpa Wilson had traveled minutes earlier.

The plan wasn't as convoluted for Micah and Katie once they arrived at the hospital emergency room. Grandpa Wilson was still being evaluated. Same department. Different rooms. Same family waiting area.

It was Brogan who won the race for a diagnosis—torn meniscus in his knee and sprained ankle. He was given crutches, higher-tech ice packs, a prescription for some pain medicine, and a firm recommendation that he see an orthopedic surgeon within the next week, if not sooner. And he was wished a merry Christmas by some of the staff, happy holidays by others, and was wheeled out of the exam room sporting a red and faux-ermine Santa hat to match his pajama bottoms.

Most of the Binder family met him in the hall outside the waiting area with a cocktail of sympathy swirled with ribbing. The pain medicine he'd been given in the exam room had started to kick in, which mellowed his response.

Micah took Katie by the arm. "I don't know how you'd be able to get him into the house by yourself. Crutches on snow aren't easy to manage. I'll need to take him home. Grandma asked specifically for you to stay. She wants you to be her medical interpreter."

Silas stepped in. "Let me take him." His furrowed brow seemed to record the anxiety everyone bore. "I didn't talk Madeline and Mackenzie through this like I should have. It's tough enough for me. Lynda spent way too much time in places like this. I owe it to my girls to be there for them right now. I'll be back if things change with Dad, or . . ."

"Brother, you go," Tim said. He gave Silas a man-hug. "We'll keep updating. God bless you, Silas. Proud to be your brother."

With Brogan loaded into the back of the van, much more comfortable for him than the rental car, the family in the waiting area settled into waiting again.

Uncharacteristically, Uncle Paul sat with his elbows on his knees and head in his hands. Allie rubbed his back and leaned against his arm.

Grandma Dodie had found a glider rocker and was giving it a workout. She crooked her finger to call Katie over. "Is it normal that they haven't told us anything yet?"

"In one way, it's a good sign," Katie said, choosing her words carefully. "That means they're still investigating, that they're devoting their complete attention to what he needs from them right now. If there's any kind of major change, they'll tell us."

"Okay." Her voice sounded childlike. When the conversation ended, Dodie still gripped Katie's hand. She lowered herself to a chair she'd pulled to Grandma Dodie's side, steering clear of the glider's trajectory.

Micah stood with his back against the wall a few feet away, arms crossed. He thumped his heart with his fist twice and pointed toward Katie. The simple gesture filled her soul. She longed to remove the pain from his face, but knew no human was capable of that.

"Family with Mr. Binder?"

The words seemed to catch them all off guard, as if surprised by what they'd been waiting so long to hear.

"That's us," Uncle Paul said, standing and brushing at his eyes.

"All of you?" The man in dark blue scrubs with a stethoscope draped around his neck and tucked into the breast pocket held an electronic tablet.

Tim scanned the room. "This isn't all of us. But yes, we're the only ones waiting right now."

The man stepped toward Grandma Dodie. "You must be his wife."

"Yes. For sixty-one years, going on sixty-two."

"I'm Kirk Franzen. I'm consulting on your husband's case."

Grandma Dodie shook his hand and said, "You're the most prayed-for doctor in the state right now, Dr. Franzen."

His smile revealed a depth of understanding and appreciation for what he'd been told. "Couldn't be . . ."—he swallowed, his Adam's apple disappearing, then reappearing—"couldn't be more grateful for that." He looked around for an open chair. Titus offered his. Dr. Franzen pulled it close to Grandma Dodie, who'd stopped rocking.

"Your husband is a conundrum for us. With the advances in medical science, it's not often anymore that I have to tell a family we don't know what's going on. At first, we suspected stroke. But it's not following a typical stroke pattern. We've done initial heart evaluations and found nothing. CT scan showed nothing suspicious that would explain his sudden unresponsiveness and his less-than-ideal vitals. Some lab results are still pending, but what we've seen has revealed nothing that would have put him in his present state."

The family circle tightened.

"We're admitting him to CCU."

Grandma Dodie looked at Katie. She whispered, "Critical care unit."

"I'm not sure that's the right place for him, to be honest," the doctor said. "It may be that his body is . . . done. We have only a thready pulse right now. It can't stay like that for long. So, you and your family may have to make some hard decisions. He had apparently signed a DNR order that is part of his medical records."

Katie turned to Grandma Dodie to explain about "do not resuscitate" orders, but Dodie said, "Our primary care doctor talked to us about that every year when we'd see him. We figured we'd take care of that as soon as we got old. Then, one day, we realized we were."

Dr. Franzen lowered his head and smiled. "Well, he's on oxygen right now. And we have him on some medications that we hope will regulate his heartbeat, but of course we have no guarantees. He hasn't responded to them at this point. No extreme measures? No life support?"

The words had the power to crush a human heart. A collective inhale made it feel as if the walls were drawing a deep breath too.

Grandma Dodie's chin quivered as she said, "That's what he wanted."

"It will take the team a little while to get him settled into the room and hooked up to the monitors. Initially, you can all see him for two minutes until you've each had a chance to say whatever you want to say to him. But I have to tell you, although it's possible, it's unlikely he can hear you at this point." He looked around the room. "Say whatever it is you want to say anyway, okay?"

Heads nodded.

"After that initial round of visits, no more than two people for ten minutes each hour. Unless we can tell he's fail— We can discuss that later. Have you had anything to eat? You might want to do that now while he's being admitted."

"Thank you" resonated around the room.

"A nurse will be out in a few minutes with Mr. Binder's room number and directions to the CCU. There's a vending machine right down this hall. Sorry, folks. But not much close by is open tonight, and the hospital cafeteria closed an hour ago. It's Christmas Eve."

The Binder Family Christmas. So far from what Katie expected, in every way.

Uncle Paul returned from his fact-finding mission pushing a small, wheeled stainless steel cart.

"Where did you get that?" Tim asked.

"From the vending machines." He pointed to a curious array of items.

"He means the cart." Deb approached cautiously, as did the other Binder women.

"Found it in the hall."

"Do you know what might have been on that cart, Paul?" Micah held his stomach.

"And that's why I lined it with paper towels."

"Where'd you get the paper towels?"

"Too many questions. Are you ready for your turkey dinner?"

"Oh, my beautiful turkeys." Grandma Dodie clasped her hands to her heart. Rhonda helped her out of her chair and assured her they were well taken care of by the team at home.

The new mom with a babe in each arm. The guy on crutches. The single dad. Two college students and five noisy little girls. Katie imagined Bella and Elisa would be two tired young women by the end of the night.

"We've got your Christmas-in-a-stable artistic interpretation of Christmas Eve dinner, people." Paul draped a paper towel over his arm. "The chef's special this evening is turkey and wilted lettuce sandwiches on desiccated bread . . ."

"Does he know desiccated means dried out?" Katie asked Micah.

"Oh, he knows."

"And," Paul continued, "another staple of Christmas dinner, cranberry sauce in its liquid form."

Tim picked up one of the cans of vending machine cranberry juice.

"I couldn't find mashed potatoes, unfortunately. But," Paul said, finger in the air like an inventor with his eureka moment, "we do have potato chips and voilà!" He pounded his palm on one of the bags. "Now mashed."

Even Grandma Dodie smiled a little with that one. "You can leave mine whole," she told him.

"So much for authenticity." Uncle Paul slid a dozen small bags of potato chips to the side. "And for dessert, a modern twist on Grandma Dodie's pecan pies. I call it Heritage Salted Nut Rolls. Bon appétit!"

Allie gave her husband a hug from behind. "You do know I adore you?"

Paul covered her arms with his. "Yes."

"And that your daughters think you're one string shy of a full box of tinsel?"

"Astute young women." Paul handed his wife a cellophane-wrapped turkey sandwich and a bag of chips. "Everyone! Time for feasting." He looked up. Katie could imagine what he was thinking as his eyes pooled with tears. Somewhere on a floor above them, a father, grandfather, husband, great-grandfather lay unresponsive. Perhaps inching his way toward an endless Christmas in the presence of the One this night honored.

Paul's face twisted. He turned away from the family and sobbed quietly in Allie's arms.

Like those community-minded silver fish in the ocean, the rest of the Binders circled around him. Micah drew Katie into the circle. She clung to him and to the power of love.

Katie had one hand on Micah's chest, so she both felt the vibrations and heard the words when Micah began to sing. "Silent Night." Katie wished she'd memorized the words to "All Is Well." She hummed the lullaby-like melody she'd heard playing repeatedly in the background in the Binder cottage over the last days. No words. Just inexplicable peace.

The cranberry juice tasted a lot like licking aluminum foil. Katie asked if anyone else wanted bottled water and turned toward the hall with the vending machines. Before she'd taken three steps, she heard, "Family for Mr. Binder?" The nurse pronounced it Bye-nder, like a three-ring binder.

Grandma Dodie asked, "Wilson?"

The nurse checked her notes. "Yes. Are you his family?"

"We are."

"I'm so sorry to have kept you waiting this long. We had a little incident getting your husband transferred, Mrs. Binder. Almost lost him. But he's a little more stable now. Here's the room number." She handed Grandma Dodie a postcard of information with a room number written in permanent marker. "Dr. Franzen will meet you in the family conference room on that floor before you go in. It's"—she looked around at the hovering family—"not a large room."

"We fold up pretty small," Paul said.

Grandma Binder thanked the nurse. The family quickly disposed of the remnants of their Christmas Eve meal and retrieved their coats and hats from the waiting room coatrack before heading for the elevators that would take them to the Critical Care Unit.

They crammed into one elevator. Katie glanced at the Maximum Capacity sign and counted heads. Oh well. Togetherness counted for a lot at times like this.

Dr. Franzen waved them into the family conference room. Sardines would have had more elbowroom if they had elbows.

"You have a lot of support, don't you, Mrs. Binder?"

"The most"—she pointed to the sardines—"and the best."

"I know this isn't what you want to hear," Dr. Franzen said. "But I also know you want me to be honest with you about your husband's condition."

"Yes. Please tell us what's going on."

Dr. Franzen put his hand on Grandma Dodie's shoulder. He scanned the room. "We can introduce life support systems temporarily, intubate him, force his heart to keep beating, and try to keep him alive until the day after tomorrow. No one wants to have Christmas Eve or Christmas Day forever be remembered as the day their loved one passed."

A harmony of gasps sucked all the air from the room.

Grandma Dodie patted the doctor's hand where it rested on her shoulder. "We've known for the last twenty-eight years, when my brother died, that every Christmas could be our last, that every moment could be the last we share together. We should have known it sooner than that. Slow learners, I guess."

"I've had a total of ten minutes with you and already know you're a remarkable family." Dr. Franzen tried to catch everyone's gaze. Katie had a mental list of ten or twelve doctors she'd like to send to Dr. Franzen for lessons on "dealing with the family."

"I wish I could have known your husband, Mrs. Binder."

"I do too. He would have liked you." She drew a deep breath. "Could I have a few minutes with my family? Would you kindly stay nearby?"

"I'll be at the nurses' station. I wish I could have brought you better news this night. Tidings of great joy seem a more appropriate announcement on a night like this. I'm so sorry."

Three Binders had to leave the room so Dr. Franzen could exit. When the family was alone, Grandma Dodie drew a breath and said, "Now, I need to say something that might not sit well with you."

"Grandma," Tim said, "I think we already know what it is."

"Does anyone have a phone?" she asked. "We need to get Silas in on this."

Eight phones volunteered. Grandma Dodie picked Titus to make the call. He filled his brother in on what the doctor said, then put Silas on speakerphone.

"Can you hear me, son?"

"I can hear you fine, Mom. I came into the mudroom. It's quieter in here."

Katie knew the feeling.

Grandma Dodie took another full-chest breath, as if getting ready to jump off a high dive. "Hear me out, please? I believe we should allow Wilson the dignity and honor of dying on the day Christ was born. An indelible new memory. Other families might have a different way of looking at it. But I don't see the point in prolonging this until a different date on the calendar, an ordinary day. He was, is, no ordinary man. For him to die on the day we celebrate that Jesus came to give us life . . . It seems fitting. Right?"

The roomful nodded or voiced their sober agreement. Silas added his yes, his voice tight, strained.

"Thank you. Now, would one of you pray, then we'll let Dr. Franzen know?"

Paul, the eldest tried, but only got through "Father God, we—" before he broke down. Tim picked up the reins. When his voice faded, Titus added the "Amen."

Grandma Dodie exhaled loudly. "Okay, then. Silas, you'll tell the others?"

"I will."

Dr. Franzen didn't disagree with their decision. "We expect the worst, but hope and pray for the best. Do you want me to wait to discontinue the medications and other equipment until the family members still at home can get here to say their final good-byes, in case that is what we're facing?"

"Boys, what's the last thing you said to your father?"

"I love you."

"I love you."

"I love you. Did you have onions for lunch, Dad?"

"Paul Stephen Binder!" Grandma Dodie turned to Dr. Franzen. "We don't leave unfinished business. There are nine more of us at home right now, seven if you don't count the babies. All who can talk know Wilson loved them. And he knows they love him. Nothing left unsaid."

Dr. Franzen lowered his head for a moment. He looked Grandma Dodie in the eye and said, "I'll write the orders to discontinue his medications and the oxygen. If he shows signs of discomfort or agitation, we'll make sure his pain is covered. You can go in and see him now."

"All of us?"

"All of you. The rules change for these last hours."

Dr. Franzen led the way to the room where Grandpa Wilson lay, then left the family alone with him.

The monitors registering his respirations, heart rate, pulse ox, and blood pressure caught Katie's attention. She didn't like what she saw. A life ebbing away.

CHAPTER ELEVEN

"Katie, you know what to expect, don't you," Grandma Dodie said after the nurse left the room with the IV pumps. "You know what's likely to happen now."

She nodded.

"Will you stay, please?"

Grandma Dodie had heard the others talking about taking shifts to give Courtney a break and let Silas come back, now that they knew it was likely the end was near. Katie considered herself the least likely candidate to remain at Grandpa Wilson's bedside for the vigil. She'd ached over the thought. Being there for Micah and his family's Christmas was what compelled her to come to Stillwater in the first place.

"It would mean a lot to Mom," Tim said. "To all of us."

Deb took both of Katie's hands. "Do you think it will be hours? Or minutes? Allie and I will go and let Courtney and Silas be part of this if you think there's time."

Katie saw her Micah in Deb's eyes. This incredibly sensitive and warmhearted woman came as part of the package for anyone who agreed to be Micah's wife. "I don't know. He's still breathing, even without the oxygen. But I wouldn't dare guess."

Tim stepped out of the room to call the cottage and inform the rest of the family about what was happening, which was nothing. No change. He returned with four folding chairs to add to the chairs a nurses' aide had already added to the small room. With most of the equipment gone, it felt like sitting around the bonfire, waiting for the flames to turn to embers and the embers to dust.

Some stood, holding Grandpa Wilson's limp hand or stroking his colorless forehead. Grandma Dodie's softer vinyl chair had been positioned at his bedside. She never let go of his hand.

"We were in this for the long haul, weren't we, Wilson?" She laid her head on the bed, her silver hair brushing his arm.

An hour passed with no change in the faint blips on the monitor. Two hours. Spent coffee cups and water bottles filled the wastebasket, and family members drifted in and out of exhausted sleep. Minutes' worth at a time.

Bathroom breaks were less complicated than at the cottage, but still carefully timed. No one wanted to leave for long, or leave Grandma Dodie alone.

When Micah left the room in search of more coffee, Katie pulled her folding chair close to her pre-fiancé's grandmother. She put her arm around the rounded shoulders. "It's an honor to be a part of this. Thank you for including me in such a tender family moment."

"You are family, Katie. Even if you're not ready to admit it yet." Grandma Dodie smiled.

"I have a few issues to reconcile before I can—"

"Your ancestry."

"That's one of them." They kept their voices low because of the solemnness in the room and the sleeping vigil-keepers, as well as the subject matter.

"Micah told me a little about that. Not sure why you'd think that disqualifies you from having a good marriage. No reason Jesus' birth should have worked out at all, considering His lineage. Generation after generation of people who either didn't know God or who messed up in a big enough way to get their stories in the Bible as 'what not to do.'"

Katie laid her head on Dodie's soft shoulder. "Unlike my family line, a couple of them behaved themselves."

"Even the best of them had their not-so-pretty moments. Like the two of us."

"You and Grandpa Wilson?"

"He almost became my ex-husband." She stroked his blue-veined hand. "Shortly after Paul was born. Wilson developed a friendship with a woman at work that went further than either of them anticipated."

Katie fought for breath. "Did you . . . leave him? Did he leave you?"

"For six months. Then we both decided if we were in it for the long haul we'd better figure out how to make that happen."

"And you did."

"That's what love, the right kind of stubbornness—and a whole lot of prayer—does for a couple." She turned her attention toward her husband again. "That ring Micah gave you, the one patterned after this one?" She held her fleshier hand toward Katie. The ring had dug a permanent impression in her finger. "This isn't," Dodie said, "the original. I had a simple gold band when we married."

The ring. She'd forgotten to tell Micah she'd dug it out from under the washing machine. And kept it with her things. "What happened to your original?"

"I threw it away."

Katie felt the blow of those words deep in her core.

"And almost threw away the marriage."

"I'm sure you thought you had every right," Katie said. A lame response. What does someone say to a statement like that?

"Wilson gave me this a year after our renewed commitment to what the first one should have represented—the two of us, no matter what, forever. I don't know if you recognized the pattern of my silverware. Eternally Yours. I bought it, piece by piece as we could afford them, over the course of the next thirty years. It meant something every time. When we say grace over a meal, it means something far more than most people know."

In it for the long haul. No matter what.

"Contentment showed up later than forgiveness. But it came. I think it's been the hardest on him. He finally admitted a few years ago that he probably did need the antidepressants our doctor had mentioned more than once."

Micah returned with coffee and cellophane-wrapped doughnuts. The crinkling was enough to wake the sleeping. All except for Grandpa Wilson, whose vitals and breathing remained unchanged.

Another hour passed, one slow second at a time.

"It's after midnight." Paul stood and made his way to the bedside. "Merry Christmas, Dad." He leaned down to kiss him.

"Merry Christmas, everybody." The greeting circled the room, husbands and wives leaning on one another.

Micah had just bitten into a powdered sugar doughnut. He set it aside and reached for Katie. She waved him off. "I'll wait."

A male voice said, "Not long, I hope."

The room stilled.

"Paul, are you practicing ventriloquism again?" Rhonda took a tentative step forward.

"No." His voice gravelly, Paul said, "It was Dad."

Grandma Dodie sat wide-eyed, speechless.

Katie glanced at the monitors and stepped to the bedside. She touched her palm to Grandpa Wilson's cheek.

"You need mittens, young lady." Grandpa Wilson's mouth quirked.

Grandma Dodie knocked over her chair in an effort to stand. "Wilson!"

In a weak but distinct voice, he said, "Something's gone a-pumpernickel."

"What did you say?"

"Something's gone a-pumpernickel. It never really goes a-rye." His eyes blinked, then closed again. "Got that from Paul. I suppose you could tell."

Allie ran for the nurse. Katie checked his pupils, felt his pulse, and stared dumbfounded at the readings on the monitors. Every level had begun to creep toward normal. A long, slow crawl, but definitely upward.

The Binders seemed caught between joy and disbelief. What just happened?

Grandpa Wilson drifted off again, but only for a moment. When the nurse came in, he managed a small wink.

As the nurse repeated the process Katie had followed, she asked, "Sir, can you tell me your name?"

"Wilson. Binder. And these are"—he raised his hand slowly—"all mine." His voice dropped so low, the nurse had to lean in to hear him.

"What did he say?" Paul asked her.

"I don't know what this means," she said, "but he was trying to sing. Something like, 'The earth will soon dissolve like snow.' Does that mean anything to you?"

Grandma Dodie clasped her hands together as if in prayer and pressed them to her mouth with a repressed sob.

"Yeah," Paul said, nodding. It took a moment to compose himself, then he recited, 'The earth will soon dissolve like snow, the sun forbear to shine; but God, who called me here below, will be forever mine.' 'Amazing Grace.'"

The nurse looked around the room. "I don't think Dr. Franzen would mind if I woke him to see this. I'll be right back. In the meantime, enjoy the moment."

Grandma Dodie leaned in to kiss her husband on the cheek. "We do. We always do."

"So," Wilson said, eyes closed but heart aimed at his wife, "what did you get me for Christmas this year?"

"I'm giving you patience."

"That's what you gave me last year, Dodie."

"Take it or leave it."

"I'll take it."

"Micah, you look so sober. Aren't you thrilled?" Katie swirled the last half-inch of coffee in the Styrofoam cup. Sludge.

Micah massaged his temples. "Of course. But it made me all the more conscious of how close we all walk to that edge—here, or gone. The next time may be the last time for him." He turned to the wall so no one else would hear. "Is it wrong to wonder if this recovery is temporary?"

"Let's wait to see what the doctor thinks before we pre-worry, okay?"

Micah smiled and traced his finger down her arm. "That sounds like something I'd say to you."

"Well!" Dr. Franzen stood in the doorway, arms crossed. "Merry Christmas to the Binder family."

"Hope your bed was more comfortable than this one, Doc." Grandpa Wilson's rasp got the words out, but barely.

Dr. Franzen ran his hand through his hair, then retraced his steps to the entrance of the room and squirted waterless hand-cleaner into his palms. "Cot in the staff lounge. And no. You got the premium bed, Mr. Wilson." He started his assessment while the family watched. "We haven't met, officially. I'm Kirk Franzen. Can you squeeze my hand? I've had the privilege of monitoring your case this evening. Now this hand? Good. Can you take a deep breath for me? Don't worry about that. After what you've been through, we'll call that deep enough for now."

"What have I been through? Apparently I slept through most of it." Grandpa Wilson's weak voice showed a small but meaningful improvement the more alert he became.

"The word sleep would be generous. And we're still not sure what brought this on, which is disconcerting. We'd like to be able to prevent another occurrence. I'm sure your family would agree."

A thought nagged at Katie. She replayed the scene with the paramedics. They'd asked about his medications. Grandma Dodie sent her to the kitchen cupboard. A zippered plastic bag held her medications. Another was marked with his name. She grabbed it and . . . and there was a single prescription bottle behind the bag. She'd assumed since it wasn't in one of the bags, it was not used regularly, not part of the everyday routine. What if—?

She'd listed the prescriptions to the paramedics, who took the bag from her. No antidepressant was among them.

"Excuse me?" She might have overlooked it. It was a grabbing-at-straws thought.

"What is it, Katie?" Grandma Dodie rubbed a hand on her bad hip.

Katie drew close to the bed. Was this even public knowledge? "Didn't you say Grandpa Wilson takes an anti-depressant?"

"Yes. This last one they tried has worked the best."

"A lifesaver," Grandpa Wilson said. "Makes me sleepier than I want to be, though. Especially with so much happening."

Dr. Franzen's eyebrows arched. "A new antidepressant? Which one?"

"I don't remember the name of it. Do you, Wilson?"

Dr. Franzen listed three or four.

"That's it. That last one," Wilson said.

"When did you start the new medication?"

Grandpa Wilson looked at his wife. She answered, "Late last week. Thursday? Yes, it was Thursday because we had to wait to pick up the hams until after we got done at the pharmacy."

"What dosage are you taking?" Dr. Franzen asked.

Grandma Dodie frowned. "We should know this. I need to update the list he carries in his wallet. All I know is the color and that he's supposed to cut them in half. The pharmacy didn't have the right strength in stock."

Grandpa Wilson's eyebrows crept up his forehead. "Cut them in half?"

"Wilson, you have been cutting them in half, haven't you? It says so right on the bottle."

Dr. Franzen leaned on the hospital bed with two fists.

"Could that have caused this?" Katie asked.

The doctor nodded his head. "Most definitely. No reversal agent. No blood levels would have told us that's what caused the symptoms. If you've inadvertently been taking twice what your doctor recommended— That could be it, folks."

"I haven't felt right for a while. Thought I'd wait until after the holidays to mention it," Grandpa Wilson said, his words clouded with remorse. "Didn't want my troubles to get in the way of Christmas."

"Good job with that plan, Dad," Paul said. The laughter that filled the room quickly faded out of respect for other patients on the unit.

"So," Grandpa said, "can we take this party and go home?"

"Not quite so fast." Dr. Franzen pointed to the monitors. "Your numbers are looking better and better. But I need to run some more labs, and we should keep an eye on things for a good part of the day. Sending you home prematurely wouldn't be wise. I pulled a forty-eight, so I'll be here all day." He crossed his arms. "Binder family, I think you got your Christmas miracle."

"We do every year." Grandma Dodie put her hand—pledge-of-allegiance style—over her heart.

"I'll dictate some orders, then I plan on getting some more shut-eye. It looks as if at least half a dozen of you would benefit from the same. If I were you, I'd go home, get some sleep. Rest assured we'll call if there's any change. Which I don't expect." Dr. Franzen turned to go with a dance move that looked like a football player in the end zone silently thanking his Creator.

"Let me stay," Paul said. "The rest of you go on home. Mom, you need to give that leg a rest. And Tim, the dark circles under your eyes have drooped to your moustache."

"I don't have a—" He rubbed above his lip. "Ooh. Maybe I do."

They gave Grandpa Wilson good night hugs, each one praying a blessing over him this time. "We'll see you later."

"I'll be here."

A beautiful benediction.

They left a vehicle for Paul, in case by some act of mercy, Grandpa Wilson was discharged before the swirling circle of silver fish made it back to the hospital. That meant the other cars were maxed out for the trip home. It gave new meaning to the phrase "lean on me."

Katie leaned against the headrest. Two a.m. on Christmas morning. Dawn would come too soon. But rivers of light already flowed around obstacles in her mind. Many years ago, Micah's grandparents' marriage had almost dissolved, and for good reason. But they fought for their marriage and won. The perfection she'd thought exquisite but unattainable wasn't perfection at all. It was a family that dug in their heels and determined to love, to survive, to repair the damaged fabric of their legacy, with God's help.

Maybe that was the definition of perfection after all. Outrageous, extravagant love.

Christmas's version—an unwed teen mother. An unexpectantly expectant father. A divine Babe in a rude manger. Perfection.

Had her resentments about her parents' and grandparents' and great-times-a-hundred-grandparents' histories kept her from fully embracing the wonder of the Christmas story all this time?

Every year when November turned to December, she tensed, expecting conflict, anticipating disappointment, waiting for more family disintegration at the holidays. And she thought she had no choice. Predisposed to relationship failure.

What if—?

"Katie. Katie?"

That deep, soothing, warm-toned voice. Micah. She opened her eyes.

"We're home," he said, nudging her from half-sleep. When he opened the car door, a blast of cold air stung her face. "Come on. There's a lovely window seat and a couple of pillows waiting for you. And frankly, my couch is going to feel like heaven tonight. What's left of the night."

Katie saw no need to find her pajamas in the dark, but climbed into her quilt nest fully clothed. She faintly heard Grandma Dodie say she was taking Paul's spot. Adapt and adjust. Binders sliding over to make room for one more. Momentary peace. Babies quiet. Silent night. Holy ni . . .

Cinnamon. She smelled cinnamon. And wood smoke. And coffee.

Katie opened one eye. Grandma Dodie and Rhonda stood a foot from her window seat. One held a plate-sized cinnamon roll, steam rising from its fluffy delightfulness. The other held an enormous holly-themed mug.

"I told you that would get to her," Rhonda said.

Katie sat up. "What time is it?"

"Nine. We can't hold off the little ones much longer. Rhonda, let's leave her breakfast on the table and let the woman have a moment to collect herself."

She scooted through the kitchen and across the corner of the family room toward the hallway but stopped halfway and backtracked. A fire crackled in the fireplace. The tree stood tall, proud, well-lit, and fragrant. Most of the family was dressed and sitting in a misshapen circle around the room, the youngest in their Christmas pajamas. But no presents sat under the tree. Hmm. She'd assumed they'd appear on Christmas morning—another Binder tradition.

Katie waved a quick greeting to the family and prayed the bathroom was unoccupied. It was.

"How do you do that?" Micah asked when she emerged ten minutes later and joined the crowd.

"Do what?"

"Look so beautiful after the kind of day we had yesterday?"

Katie smiled and sank onto one of the couches beside him. "You don't have your contacts in yet, do you?"

"I don't wear contacts."

"Must be some other explanation then. My cinnamon roll!" They must have had something to eat the day before. Hadn't they? Some details were still foggy. But her stomach felt more hollow than it had been since she'd arrived in Stillwater.

"I'll get it for you," Micah said.

"Any word from the hospital?" Katie directed her question to the bevy of adults gathered.

"Grandma Dodie talked to him this morning," Brogan said, crutching his way into the room with a duffel bag in one hand and a diaper bag over his shoulder. "Still looking good for his being released later today." He dropped the bags near the door. "Shortly after Grandpa Wilson gets here, Courtney and I are heading to my mom's. She hasn't met Evan and Gabe yet, and I'm a"—he used one crutch to point to his injured leg—"tripping hazard here."

Courtney followed with one infant in a swaddling carrier and another over her shoulder. "We'll be back for New Year's," she said. Multiple hands offered to relieve her of one of the babies. "Even if I have to come alone and let Brogan get some TLC from his mom. I'm a little . . . distracted at the moment."

"And sleep deprived and exhausted and—"

Courtney stuck one hand onto her hip, a stance that looked especially comedic with the bundle strapped to her midsection.

"And . . . the . . . very best mommy in the whole wide world!" Brogan concluded.

Micah returned with Katie's cinnamon roll and coffee, reheated for her. "Did you see how it's coming down out there? Anyone catch a weather forecast?"

Half a dozen phones appeared. Fingers punched weather apps. Almost in unison, they said, "Whoa, that doesn't look good."

Grandma Dodie stopped the cacophony like a concertmaster. "One of you. We need one of you to report. And then . . . the phones go back in the bin, okay?"

"Yes, ma'am." Tim read, "Up to ten inches of new snow before morning. Dangerously high winds predicted starting midday. Watch for drifting and whiteout conditions. Roads will be snow-covered and slippery. Hunker down, folks."

"It says 'hunker down'?" Grandma Dodie peered over her son's shoulder.

Courtney and Brogan didn't look happy about the news.

"We'd better get packed up and leave as soon as we can, Courtney."

"And miss all the— You're right. I don't like it, but we have our sons to consider now. What happened to our adventurous spirit?" Her voice sounded light, but her face registered her disappointment.

Deb wrapped her arms around her daughter. "You'll have plenty of adventure in your future. Trust me. What can I do to help?"

"Grandma Dodie, we've been waiting," Twilight said, as close to a whine as Katie had heard from anyone in their family.

Katie had wondered how long it would take for the younger ones to fidget about their long-delayed presents. Micah had insisted there was no need for Katie to get small gifts for the girls, or his parents or grandparents. She balked, but her financial picture expressed its gratitude. Now she wondered if the Binders somehow maintained a moratorium on gifts the way they had technology.

"You have been waiting a good long while, haven't you?" Grandma Dodie opened a door on an end table and pulled out a basket. "It's time. Is there anyone who hasn't yet deposited their cell phone in the technology time-out bin?"

Four sheepish hands.

"We need someone to take a video of this so Grandpa Wilson and Uncle Paul can see it later. Courtney? Brogan? Can we take a moment for this first, and get some pictures of the family, all that are here?"

"Sure. We don't want to miss this."

"It's Sunburst's turn to do the drawing," Grandma Dodie said.

Katie leaned into Micah. "What's this?"

"Our alternative to gifts under the tree. Each family

contributes toward a collection we share with a different charity every year."

"I didn't know that meant the younger children too."

"They're the most enthusiastic. I think it was Madeline's idea originally," Micah said.

"I love this family."

"Me too. Everybody writes down their charity-of-choice for the year and we pick one to be the recipient. Binder Family Tradition." Micah added, "The girls get their fair share of gifts from their parents, rest assured."

Sunburst trotted to where Grandma Binder held the basket. She dug her hand into the pieces of paper in the container, then cleared her throat. "And the winner is . . . the Every Hungry Child Fed Initiative!" Sunburst danced as the room erupted in applause and whoops. Her sisters and cousins joined her.

"Great organization," Tim said. "That reminds me . . . are there any cinnamon rolls left?"

"Timothy." Grandma Binder's tone lightened. "Yes. Plenty. But don't spoil your lunch. We have to fit a turkey dinner and ham for supper into the same day."

"It'll be rough," Tim said. "I'm not going to lie. But I'll give it my best shot. Who's with me?"

Katie didn't want to step on toes, but the solution seemed obvious. "Could we have leftovers for supper tonight and save the hams for tomorrow? Keep Christmas going? It doesn't have to end." Did she just say that?

"We can celebrate the day Jesus was one day old!" Twilight said, her enthusiastic tiptoe-response an obvious carryover from her Sugar Plum Fairy performance. "And then, the next day, when the Baby was two days old—"

"This could go on forever." Titus sighed.

Grandma Dodie's line of sight drifted to somewhere beyond the ceiling. "Would that be so bad?"

Aurora tugged on her grandmother's sleeve. "How much, Grandma? How much did we raise for the hungry children?"

"Your uncle Paul kept track of the money. We'll have to find out from him later."

"Or you could ask me now." Paul walked his father into the room from the kitchen, Wilson attempting to shake off his assistance.

"Paul Stephen Binder! You rascal! Did you know when I called that they were discharging Dad this early?" Dodie wrapped her arms around her husband and gave him a kiss that elicited another round of applause from the little girls.

Brogan tried to work the footrest to extricate his body from Wilson's chair. Grandpa Wilson waved him off and lowered himself into the kitchen chair Tim pulled from the other room.

"I talked the medical staff into it when we heard the updated forecast," Paul said. "Thought that was supposed to wait until tomorrow. Guess it was in a hurry for Christmas too."

"What are the roads like now?" Brogan asked.

"Not bad." Uncle Paul said. He felt the end of his nose and asked Aurora, "Does my nose look longer to you?"

Grandpa Wilson shook his head. "Feared for my life. The boy can find a snowdrift where there aren't any."

"I learned from the best, old man. Remember, you've been ordered to bed rest, at least for most of the day."

"I heard. I heard. Give me just a minute or two with the loves of my life."

Katie watched his kind eyes grow glossy with tears. One by one, from the youngest to the oldest, his family members gathered around him and told him how much they loved him.

"We couldn't have Christmas without you, Grandpa," Mackenzie said.

He drew her into a one-armed hug. "Christmas is going to come whether I'm here or not, you know. It's relentless that way. Nothing stopped it that first Christmas. Nothing will stop it now."

His wisdom was punctuated by winter drama.

The lights went out.

Wilson felt one small ping in his heart. And it wasn't from too much medicine. This family was going to have Christmas without him someday. The Binders would go on without him. And someday, without his Dodie. *God, if it's all the same to you, me first, okay?*

How does a man imagine life without a love like hers?

CHAPTER TWELVE

"Okay, team." Paul brushed dust from his palms. "Your ingenious uncles have the generator figured out. It'll keep the power on, but not full force. We don't know how long we'll be without electricity or how long fuel for the generator will hold out. So, limit your use of anything unnecessary. We have the stone fireplace going in the barn addition. That thing's big enough to heat the whole place out there. But we don't want anybody going out to the building alone, understand?" He drew an imaginary line from Elisa down to Twilight, stopping at every other girl in between.

"Can we tie a rope from the house to the barn, Pa? Just like on *Little House on the Prairie* on TV?" Elisa split her hair into temporary pigtails.

"Yes. And watch that long hair around these candles. 'Pa' has seen enough of hospitals for a while."

"Not kidding, girls," Tim said. "We have at least four new inches of snow already and it's blowing like crazy. We'd make you all stay in here, but it's actually warmer in the addition right now."

Katie had held her breath until Courtney called to say they'd made it to Brogan's mom's house in Hudson. Not a long trip, but the new mom insinuated she'd be more than a little grateful when Brogan could drive again. The babies slept the whole way, which Courtney pronounced a gift. She reported that all of Stillwater was without power, but Hudson, a little south and across the river, still functioned.

With Micah's sister and little ones safely in Hudson, the great-grandparents reclaimed the master bedroom. Grandpa Wilson took his obligatory nap, but Grandma Dodie busied herself in the kitchen, the exhaustion of Christmas Eve replaced by the adrenalin of prepping for Christmas dinner with generator power only. "How does everyone feel about cold turkey sandwiches?" she called out.

"And canned cranberry juice?" Titus asked.

"Sorry, son. You'll have to make do with homemade cranberry sauce."

Katie folded the quilts from her nest, then thought better of it and deposited them in the family room. They might be needed if the fireplace couldn't keep up and the generator failed. What a difference a few thousand miles made. Florida used generators to keep things cool when the power went out.

Titus bundled his girls for a trip to the barn addition. Mackenzie and Madeline suited up too. Silas reminded them about scarves and to pull their hoods over their hats. "They want one more practice for their annual Christmas pageant.

And apparently, it's top secret again," he said to the adults. "What time do you want us back for the meal, Mom?"

"I'm aiming for one. Oh, Silas?"

"Yes?"

"I have a stack of paper plates in the storage cupboard out there. Seems like the occasion calls for them."

Bella and Elisa grabbed their coats and boots. "We were cast as angels' assistants this year. We'll keep them out of trouble. Comes with the role."

"Bless you two. I raised you well," Paul said.

"It was mostly Mom's influence," Elisa said, dodging her father's lunge on their way to the back door.

The kitchen appeared cozier than ever with the lights low and without the typical noises of mixers and outdated dishwasher. The generator would keep the necessaries functioning. But Grandma Dodie declared the washer and dryer, microwave, and several other appliances off-limits. Even the conversation dimmed with the reduced power.

"What's the longest you've been without power during a storm like this?" Katie asked, peering out at her first blizzard. The snow that had been gentle and picturesque before now pelted and careened. Directionless, it changed its mind with every gust of wind. The low howl the wind made reminded her of the kind of scary movies she refused to watch. Yet, through the melee of gusts and snow, light from the barn addition broke through, as holy light from an ancient stable must have lit Bethlehem millennia ago.

"What year was it, Grandma Dodie, that we didn't get power restored for almost two weeks?" Allie asked.

Two weeks?

"Don't scare the woman, Allie. One of the boys checked the long-term forecast. Admittedly, that technology came in handy. When the phones all die out, we'll find the old radio we used to listen to. It's a fierce but short-lived storm, or so the weathercasters say. Midday tomorrow it should calm down. We never know how long it will be before power can be restored. Depends."

She made her pronouncements so calmly, as if the disruption to her plans couldn't faze her. Katie thought again of the woman on the sidewalk outside of LoLo's—the woman allergic to changes in her plans.

"How can I help with the meal?" Katie squirted waterless cleaner on her hands and rubbed them dry.

"Can you figure out a way to boil potatoes without an electric stove?" Dodie asked. "I told Wilson our next major purchase should be a gas stove."

"If we were on the beach," Katie said, "we'd wrap them in foil and tuck them into the embers in the fire."

"Could work," Allie said. "Between the fireplace here and the one in the barn addition, we might be able to pull that off. Deb, are you okay?"

She sat at the table with her head in her hands. "I miss my grandsons. I know they'll be back in a few days. But I didn't realize how quickly I'd lose my heart to those little guys."

"This will help." Grandma Dodie handed Deb a roll of aluminum foil. "Tear off about forty squares of this."

Deb laughed. "How is this supposed to help?"

"I may have exaggerated its healing impact. But it'll help us get those spuds on the fire. Serving equals endorphins, which equals a sense of euphoria and there you go. Rhonda, back me up, here." Grandma Dodie took Deb's head in her hands and kissed her forehead. "Of all people in this room, I understand, dear. Nothing gives me more joy than having my children and grandchildren close to me, under this roof."

"Providing, of course, the roof is still standing by morning," Rhonda said.

"Rhonda!"

"It's beautiful, in a way," Katie said. "The chaos." She leaned on the sink to catch a better view.

Allie put a hand on her shoulder. "The storm?"

"That too."

"One of you want to drain these potatoes?" Grandma Dodie asked. "We need to get them wrapped and in the fire. How long should we leave them to cook?"

Katie turned to face the Binder women. "Until they're done, I guess."

The snickers started with Grandma Dodie then circled the kitchen. "So, you caught Micah's laid-back stance while you were here?" Rhonda said. "I didn't realize it was that contagious."

"He's a good influence on me."

Deb tore off another square of foil. "Don't underestimate your influence on him. We can all see it."

Katie opened her mouth to argue, but instead silently thanked God for the faint possibility that the statement was true.

The blizzard rattled windows, which no one but Katie seemed to notice. She pulled another batch of foil-wrapped potatoes from the fire, which was doing a fine job of keeping the family room warm.

"God bless whoever had the forethought to finish baking these turkeys and taking the meat off the bones yesterday," Grandma Dodie said when Katie deposited the final batch of fire-roasted potatoes into the massive mixing bowl reserved for the purpose. "The meat won't be heated up, but cold turkey that doesn't come from a vending machine works just fine for me this year."

"That would be me," Titus said, entering through the mudroom, his cheeks ruddy from the cold.

"Thank you, son."

"The turkeys helped keep my mind occupied while you were with Dad. The girls are on their way in, with their props."

Katie couldn't imagine fitting homegrown pageant props into the already overcrowded cottage. She waited for someone to object. No one did. The grace that permeated the house like air freshener in other homes extended to overly energetic girls with a flair for the dramatic.

"So, Katie, do you think these potatoes will mash up and stay warm until we're all gathered?"

"All we can do is try."

"The boys let me use the generator long enough to make gravy in the electric skillet. Isn't that something for you?" Grandma Dodie said.

"What is, Mom?" Deb asked.

"My gravy was worth the generator power, but they said it would be a waste of fuel to make the Brussels sprouts."

Katie used every bit of the energy she'd invested in strength training over the past year in mashing potatoes that smelled of wood smoke and butter.

The dressing seemed risky and not altogether pleasant to serve cold, so it sat in the refrigerator, waiting to perform as an awkward accompaniment to the next day's planned ham dinner.

With battery-operated candles interspersed among the serving bowls and platters on the tables, the holiday meal seemed ideally decorated. After all had taken their places, Grandpa Wilson said, "Let's pray." No words followed.

Dodie laid her hand over his. "Are you okay, Wilson? Is this too much for you?"

"Too little, my beloved. It will always be too little for my liking. But let's celebrate while we have it. Heavenly Father, thank You for this fam— Thank You for this family gathered around these tables. We thank You for the gift of life, and endless life through Your Son. Now bless this food and the hands that prepared it, that we might serve You all our days, however many, however few. In the Name of Jesus. Amen."

"Amen," the family chorused.

He finished his prayer by kissing his beloved on the back of her hand.

Paul picked up a platter of turkey and said, "You can't blame that one on me. Let's eat." He showed the plate to Allie and squinted. "Is this light meat or dark meat?" He flipped the switch on a camping light headband he'd pulled over his forehead. "Ah. Never mind. Light meat. Get it?"

"Uncle Paul," Elisa said, "look away. Look away! You're blinding us!"

He flicked the light off. "Told you, Allie. All the girls say I have a dazzling personality."

So it was going to be that kind of Christmas meal. Katie took the bowl passed to her, but almost didn't want to eat. She would have preferred to listen, to catch every nuance of conversation and shared banter.

"You never have to wonder, if it's tofu," Rhonda said.

Titus held a bite of turkey to his open mouth. Motionless.

"I'm just saying," she said, "that you never have to wonder if it's dark or light meat."

"Because it's not meat," Titus said. "I thought you were giving up your normal eating habits in order to enjoy this Christmas, Rhonda."

"Did I say Christmas?" She looked around the table. "I meant Lent."

"Food fight!"

"Paul Stephen Binder!"

No one went hungry. No one complained the turkey was cold. And hearts filled at least as much as stomachs, Katie guessed, judging from her own experience at this table to which she no longer considered herself an outsider. No longer a virtual orphan.

The tables were cleared by flashlight so as not to miss any stray messes. The kitchen clanged with activity as it always did at the end of a Binder meal. Several volunteered to heat water in the enormous cast-iron kettle Grandpa Wilson once used to boil maple sap into syrup. They'd need an outdoor fire, and courage to brave that kind of cold and misery. How long would it take water to boil with the snow coming down that hard?

In the end, it was decided to do the best they could for the moment and pray the snow would let up, or that they could wait at least until after the remaining traditional Christmas Day activities—the girls' pageant and Grandpa Wilson reciting the Christmas Story.

True darkness would fall early with such thick clouds blocking the zillion jigawatt sun beyond them somewhere. Mid-afternoon, and it felt like long past sunset.

With the leftovers put away in picnic coolers on shelves in the unheated part of the barn to avoid letting cold air out of the refrigerator and freezer in the cottage, the family settled into its gathering spot. Adults occupied couches and chairs now encircling the room to allow for the theater-in-the-almost-round style production of the Binder Girls Christmas Extravaganza.

The theater troupe waited in the hall while Elisa took her place as announcer in front of the fireplace and Christmas tree wall.

Katie leaned toward Micah. "This can't wait until after the weather clears?"

"Hard to rein in that kind of excitement," he said. "Besides, it's taking the girls' minds off the storm. A few adult minds too."

"The creators of this production would like me to read the following disclaimer." Elisa held the paper to the side to see the words by firelight. "We've heard the Christmas story told for many years through the shepherds' point of view. We know what the angels said. But do we know what they were thinking? No." She paused. "And you won't know after this pageant either. Because some things we can't know until Jesus tells us face-to-face."

In an aside to the crowd, Elisa said, "They wanted me to say eyeball-to-eyeball, but I edited." She flicked the paper flatter and continued. "So kindly allow us to take you on a journey to the angels' dispatch center for . . . 'The Angels' Story,' starring, from oldest to youngest, Sunburst, Mackenzie, Aurora, Madeline, and Twilight Binder, with Bella Binder serving as musical accompaniment and sound effects. The actresses have chosen to retain their own names for their angel characters, since Grandma Dodie always said our names are angelic."

The girls floated in, wearing white tunics belted with gold garland and sporting halos of glow sticks on their heads. Bella sat on the floor at the far side of the tree, almost in the hallway, a guitar in her lap.

"I didn't know Bella plays guitar," Katie whispered to Micah.

"She's really good."

He wouldn't have had to say it. From the first notes, Katie could tell Bella had a gift. She played an unfamiliar tune with light notes and sweet harmonies appropriate for an angel's dispatch center. It resonated uniquely in the candlelight and firelight.

The five youngest Binder girls stood together in a line, tapping and swiping on pieces of cardboard cut to the size and shape of electronic tablets. Each "tablet" was personally decorated on the side that faced the audience.

"Anything happening?"

"See anything new, anybody?"

"I think she's dropped." Aurora held her tablet for the other angels to see.

Snickers circled the room.

"Yes, Mary's definitely dropped," Mackenzie said. Taller than the others, she had no trouble acting the part of a convincing head angel.

"Technically, it's the Baby who dropped." Sunburst thrust her hip out and rested her hand on it, more than self-assured.

"I'll bet Mary's breathing a little better now," Madeline said.

"But she's probably getting up even more often at night," Twilight added.

Katie wondered if Rhonda had trained her girls to be midwives.

"Won't be long now," the girls said in unison.

Madeline swiped an imaginary screen on her "tablet." "I want to go tell her she's almost there," she said, her voice barely audible.

"We're all excited, Angel Madeline," Twilight said. "But you got to be the one to tickle Elizabeth's belly and make her baby jump when Mary showed up at her house."

"That was fun," Madeline said, looking wistfully heavenward, which Katie found amusing since they were supposedly in heaven at the moment.

"That was the first time Mary sang." Aurora and the other angels bowed their heads.

Silence. "Is it over already?" Katie whispered.

"Not by a long shot, if I know these girls." Micah put his arm around Katie and drew her closer.

Bella's guitar music swelled. She sang into the darkened room, "In the very depths of who I am, I rejoice in God my Savior. He has looked on me with favor, looked on me with favor . . ."

As comical as the Binder angels had been, Bella's song brought Katie into the wonder of what it must have been like to be among the cast of humans who welcomed the Savior into the world. Bella sang as the voice of a woman who couldn't believe she of all people had been chosen to carry the Christ Child. In her youth. With the scars and dings on her family history. But with a purity of heart that, no matter how difficult or socially uncomfortable or at what risk to her relationship with her betrothed, she could make only one choice—say yes to God. "I am the Lord's servant. Let it be with me just as You have said," Bella sang. "May it ever be with me just as You have said."

An unbidden thought lingered with the final notes of the song. A few days ago, Katie would have intentionally ignored it. Now, she mentally tore down remnants of resistance and invited it closer. A fully formed thought she couldn't imagine came from within her. What Christmas accomplished enables me to forgive my heritage and consider it now as dramatic contrast to who I want to be and the life I want to live. The scars and dings on Mary's family history accomplished what years of trying had been unable to do.

She didn't try to stop her tears. She didn't have to look around to know others were sniffing, too, including the man on whose shoulder she leaned.

It had been brewing, maybe even since ten months ago when Micah first asked if she wanted to go for coffee. He prayed over the coffee and their conversation. Who does that? Someone who has lived the lyrics, "May it ever be with me just as You have said, God."

Bella was "Undeclared" for her major? With a voice like that, and an ability to engage an audience, Katie had an idea for her. Had Bella written the song? So much more to learn about this family.

When Bella's song ended, and her guitar returned to mood-setting background music, the angels raised their heads, onstage again. Aurora repeated, "That was the first time Mary sang. Won't be the last."

"She'll be singing lullabies soon," Angel Mackenzie said. She waved her tablet. "I made a playlist for her."

More snickers around the room.

Sunburst switched hips and attitudes. "I wonder what Jesus will look like as a baby."

"Give me a minute." Aurora tapped the screen of her tablet. "Age-reversing software won't work on this, since He's been around since the beginning of time. But take a look at these possibilities. I made a composite of the faces of male babies from the region, assuming there will be some likeness to Mary's family line."

"You're such a geek, Angel Aurora," Angel Twilight said.

Aurora's eyes grew wide. Between clenched teeth, she said, "That's not in the script."

"I'm ad-lipping."

"Libbing."

"What?"

Mackenzie cleared her throat and adjusted her glow stick halo. "Could we see your composition?"

"Composite." The other angels gathered around Aurora, peeking over her shoulder. In sync, they each tilted their head to the left and sighed, then slowly to the right and sighed.

Paul laughed out loud. "Sorry, girls. Er, angels," he said. "Carry on."

Twilight looked at her tablet. "Oh, that's a good sign!"

"What is?" The angel troupe shifted focus to Twilight.

"They just arrived in Bethlehem. We all know the baby's supposed to be born in Bethlehem."

"Copy that. According to . . ."—Madeline tapped—"my Micah app . . ." She stopped and whispered, "Uncle Micah, did you know you were in the Bible?"

"Yes, I did," he whispered in return.

"I mean, a whole book of you?"

"He's named after that Micah," Tim said. Katie admired the man's ability to keep a straight face through that exchange.

"Oh. Cool. Here it is on my Micah app. Micah 5:2—'As for you, Bethlehem of Ephra . . . Ephrawhatever, even though you remain least among the clans of Judah, nevertheless, the one who rules in Israel for me will emerge from you. His existence has been from anti-quidity, even from eternity.'"

Mackenzie huffed. "Antiquity."

"You're not the boss of me." Madeline jumped. "Got a text. Huh."

"Me too."

"Me too."

"Me too!"

Madeline looked at her companion angels. "Where are you being assigned?"

"Some field out in the middle of nowhere. Seriously?" Sunburst dropped her shoulders. "I wanted to be assigned to Bethlehem. Where are you going?" she asked the next in line, Aurora.

"Field."

"Field."

"Field." Twilight presented a perfect pout, as if she'd rehearsed long before arriving at the cottage. "We'll miss everything!"

Aurora looked at the others. "You're not thinking about disobeying a direct order, are you?"

"We're angels. Not idiots," Twilight said.

Rhonda groaned.

Twilight walked over to her mother and said, "Mom, it's okay. It's pretend. I would never use that word for real."

Rhonda kissed her youngest on the cheek and sent her back to the scene.

"No," Twilight continued, affecting a beyond-angelic nature. "We would never disobey a direct order."

Sunburst heaved a gigantic sigh. "We'll have to DVR the birth and watch it later."

Micah coughed so hard, Katie's head bounced off his shoulder. She patted his knee.

"More incoming instructions," Sunburst said, eyeing her tablet. Her face brightened. "Ohh."

"What?" Angel Mackenzie repositioned her halo again.

"Time to rock and roll, angels," Sunburst said. "To the fields!" She extended her arm like a raised sword and led the others offstage.

Bella's guitar music swelled again. An ancient carol about shepherds watching their flocks.

The troupe of angels reappeared at the end of the song, crouched as they walked in.

"When will we know?" Madeline asked.

"We'll know." Angel Mackenzie told her.

Sunburst exaggerated her disappointment. "I wanted to be the one to tell the shepherds, 'Fear not!' I've been practicing all the way here. Listen to this." She cupped her hands around her mouth and shouted, "Fear not, for Pete's sake! This is good news!"

Katie covered her amusement as best as she could, grateful for the semi-darkness and shadows.

"Which is why"—Aurora said—"all the big parts go to the bigger angels."

A bright light shone from near the door. Elisa held a flashlight overhead, trained on the floor in the middle of the room.

The angels looked up.

"The star!"

"Oh!"

"It's almost time."

Faintly, under her breath, Mackenzie counted, "One. Two. Three," and the angels made classic surprised expressions—wide eyes, round mouths.

"Oh! The angel of the Lord is speaking!"

"What's our cue? What's our cue?" Twilight asked.

Madeline whispered, "He has to get to the part about 'and lying in a manger.' We're the 'Suddenly.'"

"Got it."

"Look at the shepherds." Aurora stood and crossed her hands over her heart. "This is like the biggest thing that's ever happened to them!"

Sunburst dragged on her sister's shoulder to get her into crouch position again. "Biggest thing that's ever happened . . . ever! Now, shhhh. We'll miss our cue."

The little girls' faces reflected the anticipation Katie felt in her own heart.

From the corner by the door, Elisa said, "And suddenly—"

The girls leapt to their full height, arms raised high. Madeline's halo slipped. She quickly righted it.

Elisa smiled but continued, "There was with the angel a multitude of the heavenly hosts, praising God and saying—"

The angelic host, perfectly synchronized, with "Hallelujah Chorus" kind of joy on their faces shouted, "Glory to God in the highest! And on earth, peace. Goodwill toward men!"

They high-fived each other and exited to the backstage hallway.

"Hey!" Twilight stuck her head around the corner. "Isn't anybody going to applaud?"

Laughter, applause, tenderness, tears . . .

The girls received hugs and kudos from their parents first, then the rest of the family.

Uncle Paul couldn't help himself. He said, "So, Madeline, they had tablets in Bible times? I don't think so." He tickled his daughter, Bella, in the ribs.

"We knew you'd say that, Dad. Elisa, show him."

Grinning, Elisa borrowed Grandpa Wilson's Bible from the end table by his chair.

"It's in Luke," Madeline said.

"I remember." Elisa flipped pages, using the "star" flashlight to find the spot. "This is Zechariah when he couldn't speak while Mary's aunt Elizabeth was expecting. And I quote . . ."

"And she quotes," Madeline said.

"'Then they began gesturing to his father to see what he wanted to call him. Zechariah asked for a tablet, and surprised everyone by writing, "His name is John."'"

Paul raised his hands in surrender. "I stand corrected. And hungry. Grandma Dodie, is there anything to eat?"

The entire Binder family groaned.

Katie sought out Bella. "I didn't know you could play and sing like that."

Bella shrugged one shoulder. "It was either do the music or wear a glow stick halo. Easy choice."

"Well, I know I'm not the only one who appreciated it, and who recognizes that you have an exceptional gift."

"Thanks."

"Did you write the first song?"

Bella nodded.

"Pretty amazing. Who wrote the script?"

"Collaboration," Bella said. "We've done a Christmas play every year since Elisa and I could both talk, I think. It got bigger and bigger with every granddaughter born."

"No parts for male characters?" Katie said, nodding toward where Micah stood.

"The year we made him the donkey, he said 'Never again.'"

Elisa joined them. "When you were fifteen," she said, "would you have appreciated putting on plays with your six-year-old and four-year-old cousins? Oh, wait a minute. That's practically what we just did."

"I didn't have a lot of interaction with my cousins growing up," Katie said. A stab of pain. It resolved more quickly than usual.

"That's too bad." Elisa turned toward the jagged line of little girls in halos. "Let's get your costumes off and props put away, angels. It's about time for the real Christmas story."

GRANDPA WILSON SETTLED into his chair, but left the footrest down, almost a necessity in a room with that many people and that little light. He pulled his Bible onto his lap.

"Do you want me to find you that flashlight, Dad?" Paul asked, already on his way to standing.

"No, son. No. This is just right."

The sense of calm in his voice quieted the undercurrent of random discussions and chatter. Peace on earth.

He peered through the dim light at the faces of his family, resting on each one for a moment. Then he drew a deep breath and, without glancing at his open Bible, announced, "The Christmas Story, as told to us by the apostle Luke. 'Because of our God's deep compassion . . .'"

"Grandpa," Madeline, who sat cross-legged at his feet, whispered. "That's not how it starts. Remember? 'And it came to pass in those days . . . ?'"

He leaned to put his hand on her head. Katie's heart ached with that simple act missing from her childhood. "The story begins long before that, little one," Grandpa Wilson said. "But today, we'll start here. 'Because of our God's deep compassion, the dawn from heaven will break upon us, to give light to those who are sitting in darkness and in the shadow of death, to guide us on the path of peace.'"

"That's us!" Twilight said in breathy awe. "Sitting in darkness."

When he paused, the whole dark room paused with him. Peace deepened. "'And it came to pass in those days that a decree went out from Caesar Augustus that all the world should be taxed. And all went to be taxed, every one into his own city. And Joseph also went up from Galilee, out of the city of Nazareth, into Judaea, unto the city of David, which is called Bethlehem; (because he was of the house and lineage of David:).'"

Micah squeezed her hand. Lineage. David's, with unsavory relatives, a father who didn't always respect him, a wife who didn't understand him, friends who loathed what he'd done when he walked away from God's plan for him. She squeezed back. *I noticed.*

"'To be taxed with Mary his espoused wife, being great with child.'" Grandpa Wilson let those words settle over them. "'And so it was, that, while they were there, the days were accomplished that she should be delivered. And she brought forth her firstborn son, and wrapped him in swaddling clothes, and laid him in a—'" He held his hand toward the two youngest.

"'Manger! Because there was no room for them in the inn.'"

That's what Katie had walked into. No room. Somehow the Binders made room for her.

"Micah?" Grandpa Wilson said, "Do you want to take it from here?"

"Me?"

"The day's coming—maybe not for a while—when you'll be sitting in a place like this, looking out over your legacy,"

Grandpa Wilson said, "telling them the unending Christmas story. I won't live to see it. But I imagine it will look and feel a lot like this. I pray it does."

Katie laid her head on Micah's arm and her hand on his heart. She wanted to feel the vibration of the words as he granted his grandfather the gift of hearing what Micah's children and grandchildren would hear.

"Do you want this?" Grandpa Wilson lifted his Bible toward him.

"No." Micah bowed his head briefly, then raised it and said, "'And there were in the same country shepherds abiding in the field, keeping watch over their flock by night. And, lo, the angel of the Lord came upon them, and the glory of the Lord shone round about them: and they were sore afraid.'"

Katie would never tire of the sound of his voice. She would . . . never . . . tire of it.

"'And the angel said unto them, Fear not: for, behold, I bring you good tidings of great joy, which shall be to all people. For unto you is born this day in the city of David a Saviour, which is Christ the Lord. And this shall be a sign unto you; Ye shall find the babe wrapped in swaddling clothes, lying in a manger.'"

The soft rustling sound turned out to be Grandma Dodie passing a box of tissues around the room. Katie let her tears fall on Micah's shirt.

"'And suddenly!'"—he said at double volume, making the little girls giggle—"'there was with the angel a multitude of the heavenly host praising God, and saying, Glory to God in the highest, and on earth peace, good will toward men.'"

A log in the fireplace settled into a new resting place, sending a spray of sparks up the chimney.

Bella began to play again, this time the song Katie had found herself singing in the dark, the one that captured her attention within minutes of being introduced to the Binder Family Christmas. "All Is Well."

As her song drew to its end, Grandpa Wilson, holding his Bible to his chest now, began to sing. Katie watched the firelit room settle once more.

Yea, when this flesh and heart shall fail,
And mortal life shall cease,
I shall possess, within the veil,
A life of joy and peace.

Why had she never realized "Amazing Grace" was as much a Christmas song as any other?

"Grandpa Binder?"

In the dim light, two Binder men answered "Yes?" which started another wave of laughter. Tim winked at his nieces. "Sorry. I've been waiting a long time to respond to that name."

"So far," Grandpa Wilson told Tim, "you can only answer when little boys call for their grandpa. So far." He made a dramatic point of directing his attention to where Micah and Katie sat before turning to answer his granddaughter. "What is it, Madeline?"

"Who's Haste?"

"Haste is when you hurry up real fast."

"Not what is it," she said. "Who. In the Bible?"

"I don't know what you mean, sweetie."

She stood and drew closer to his good ear. "You know, when the shepherds said, 'Let's go to Bethlehem, and see this thing which is come to pass. And they came with Haste, and found Mary, and Joseph, and the babe lying in a manger.' Was Haste just a friend? Or somebody important?"

"Haste is rarely a friend," Grandpa Wilson said, his wide smile visible even in the semi-darkness. "But . . . sometimes important."

Grandma Dodie spoke up. "Don't confuse the girl, Wilson. When they went 'with haste,' that just means they hurried."

The girl pondered. "Well, yeah. Who wouldn't? Even you hurried when Gabe and Evan showed up, Grandma Dodie. Imagine if we were on our way to see Jesus! Like Mom did."

Something shifted in Katie's heart. Weeks ago, a scene like this would have sent her into mourning over how far the sweetness was from the kind of family Christmas she'd known in her growing-up years.

Here, in this cramped cottage, in the middle of a blizzard, with the fragility of life all the more real and the hard roads these people had traveled far more rutted than the lane along the split-rail fence, with all plans upended and the meal a shadow of what Grandma Dodie hoped it would be, with Grandpa Wilson home but for how long, she allowed herself to feel the full impact of the enduring love that hemmed the Christmas story. The amazing grace laced through its ancient yet ever-new lines.

Grandma Dodie clapped her hands together. "Have you ever made s'mores with Christmas cookies, kids?"

Paul answered, "No! Great idea!"

Dodie *tsked.* "Paul, I was talking to the younger ones."

"Oh, the burdens of being the oldest in the family," he said, his gift for drama evident.

"We'll toast marshmallows in the fireplace," she said. But I'll need some helpers to get everything ready."

All the Binder girls volunteered and followed Grandma Dodie into the kitchen.

The four Binder sons donned coats, boots, and gloves to search for long sticks suitable for roasting marshmallows and to gather more wood for the fires. Deb, Rhonda, and Allie disappeared into the kitchen, too, Rhonda leading the charge for healthy alternatives to the marshmallows.

At that moment, the cottage seemed almost roomy, despite the way shadows and darkness can make walls close in.

"Want more coffee?" Micah asked Katie.

"Definitely."

"Be right back."

She sat on the wide hearth and waited for him. When he returned with their coffee mugs, she took his, too, and set both mugs a few feet away on the hearth. She invited him to sit beside her. "Do you still have your phone, Micah?"

"Grandma Dodie told us to get rid of them."

She tilted her head. "Do you?"

He pulled it from his pants pocket. "I was going to get to that."

Katie stood and walked to the darkened Christmas tree. She shone the light from the phone's flashlight onto a spot on the back of the tree at about eye level.

"You can't hide my phone behind the tree. She'll find it."

"Uh-huh. Here, you can have it back." Katie tossed it to him and found her way back to the hearth.

"Find what you were looking for?"

"I did." She didn't elaborate.

Micah slid closer to her. "I'm glad you came here, Katie."

"Me too."

"A whole new level of intensity this year. Would you believe me if I told you it isn't always this bad?"

She took his hand and stroked his palm. "I believe you." She pressed her find into his opened hand.

"Where'd you get that?"

"From under the washing machine." She leaned her head on his shoulder. "Micah, will you marry me? Dysfunctions and all?" She could hear his heart pounding.

"Your dysfunctions or mine?" His voice held an unusual tremble.

"I'd better say both."

He entwined his hand with hers, the ring cupped between them. The battery-operated candles in the windows flickered, but not because the wind howled outside. The fire warmed her back. His presence warmed her heart. But he didn't speak.

"Micah? You haven't said anything."

"Praying. Give me a minute."

So, now he was the one with doubts? A cold draft swept through her, despite the fire at her back.

"Amen," he said.

"Did you get the answer you needed?" Katie asked.

"I wasn't asking. I was thanking God for giving me my heart's desire." He took the ring from the space between their hands and slipped it on her ring finger. "Yes. An endless yes."

She held her hand so the ring could catch the light from the flames. "I believe the next step," she said, "is that you kiss me?"

He didn't need convincing. The hug that followed was well in excess of the necessary twenty seconds, Katie noted.

"Sorry, folks. We'll need you to do that all again," Uncle Paul said. "My cell phone died mid-taping. But Allie's still has battery power. So, from the top."

From deep in the kitchen, they heard, "Paul Stephen Binder! Don't make me come in there."

"Mom, she said yes!"

"Technically," Katie interjected, "he did."

Other Books by Cynthia Ruchti

(Non-Fiction)

Tattered and Mended: The Art of Healing the Wounded Soul

Ragged Hope: Surviving the Fallout of Other People's Choices

(Fiction)

As Waters Gone By

All My Belongings

When the Morning Glory Blooms

They Almost Always Come Home

ACKNOWLEDGMENTS

An Endless Christmas was a **Joy-to-the-World** kind of project. The idea lived only a short while in my mind before Pamela Clements and Worthy Inspired offered me the opportunity to give it voice. I'm grateful that I had the chance to meet these characters and hear their story while I was writing it.

I've been blessed with wonderful publishing teams, and the Worthy Inspired team is no exception. No matter the role each member plays, the people in those positions have made the process a delight. They **shepherd** book projects well.

Jamie Clarke Chavez served as freelance editor for this story. Jamie, I always marvel at the insights you provide and the way you ask me to dig deeper sometimes. The best finds are often the ones buried deepest. Thank you. My characters sang, **All Is Well.** It's the song I sing when working with you.

Hark, the Herald *Agents* Sing! Wendy Lawton, you and the entire Books & Such Literary Management team are a perpetual source of blessing and encouragement. Thank you for championing this story.

Do You Hear What I Hear? It's the sound of a cadre of people who go to their knees for every book I write, including this one. Please know how much I appreciate that divine attention.

When I hear the call, **O Come, All Ye Faithful,** I know I can count on my family to respond, to support and cheerlead for what I write. You are faithful, and I am grateful.

Readers, the last acknowledgment is reserved for you. You make my heart sing the **Hallelujah Chorus.** I pray you will find within these pages a story that compels you to voice your own hallelujah.

ABOUT THE AUTHOR

Drawing from thirty-three years of on-air radio ministry, Cynthia Ruchti tells stories of "hope-that-glows-in-the-dark" through her novels and novellas, nonfiction books and devotionals, and speaking for women's and writers' events. Her books have been recognized by Romantic Times Reviewers' Choice Awards, Selah Awards, the Gayle Wilson Award of Excellence, Christian Retailing's BEST Awards, and Carol Award nominations, among other honors, including a Family Fiction Readers' Choice Award. She and her plot-tweaking husband live in Pittsville, Wisconsin, not far from their three children and five grandchildren.

Visit Cynthia at www.cynthiaruchti.com

IF YOU ENJOYED THIS BOOK, WILL YOU CONSIDER SHARING THE MESSAGE WITH OTHERS?

Mention the book in a blog post or through Facebook, Twitter, Pinterest, or upload a picture through Instagram.

Recommend this book to those in your small group, book club, workplace, and classes.

Head over to facebook.com/CynthiaRuchtiReaderPage, "LIKE" the page, and post a comment as to what you enjoyed the most.

Tweet "I recommend reading #AnEndlessChristmas by @cynthiaruchti // @worthypub"

Pick up a copy for someone you know who would be challenged and encouraged by this message.

Write a book review online.

Visit us at worthypublishing.com

twitter.com/worthypub

worthypub.tumblr.com

facebook.com/worthypublishing

pinterest.com/worthypub

instagram.com/worthypub

youtube.com/worthypublishing